GHOST ISLAND AND THE MYSTERY OF CHARMANDER

AN UNOFFICIAL ADVENTURE FOR POKÉMON GO FANS

Ken A. Moore

Sky Pony Press
New York

Copyright © 2016 Skyhorse Publishing, Inc.

First Edition

This is a work of fiction. Names, characters, places, and incidents are from the authors' imaginations, and used fictitiously.

Sky Pony Press books may be purchased in bulk at special discounts for sales promotion, corporate gifts, fund-raising, or educational purposes. Special editions can also be created to specifications. For details, contact the Special Sales Department, Sky Pony Press, 307 West 36th Street, 11th Floor, New York, NY 10018 or info@skyhorsepublishing.com.

Sky Pony® is a registered trademark of Skyhorse Publishing, Inc.®, a Delaware corporation.

Visit our website at www.skyponypress.com.
Books, authors, and more at www.skyponypressblog.com

10 9 8 7 6 5 4 3 2 1

Library of Congress Control Number: 2016953551

Cover illustration by Geraldine Rodríguez
Cover design by Brian Peterson

Paperback ISBN: 978-1-5107-2296-5
Ebook ISBN: 978-1-5107-2297-2

Printed in Canada

PART ONE

The house was old. And a little bit scary. And smelled bad.

Maybe not exactly "bad," Sarah decided, but definitely old and strange. Musty. Like a place nobody had bothered to take care of in a very long time.

The front door was open. Sarah could smell the strange house-odor from all the way out on the porch. She looked up at the old wooden door-frame—the paint on it had chipped, as had the paint along the rest of the house. She took a deep breath, and moved closer.

The house was perched on the Atlantic coast on a rocky outcropping in Northern Maine in a tiny town called Clybourne. Sarah had never been before. Her twin brother, Skip, had never been there, either, as far as she knew. Their mother had once visited this strange old house, but that had been years and years ago.

For perhaps the hundredth time, Sarah wondered why their mother had decided to move them all the way across the country to this strange place in the middle of nowhere, farther north than some parts of Canada.

"Wow!" a loud voice called from just behind Sarah. "Just *look* at this place!"

Sarah quickly moved to the side as her brother raced past her into the house like an out-of-control car, before disappearing inside. Sarah steadied herself against the ancient doorframe and took a deep breath.

"Omigosh," Skip called to her from within the house. "You're never going to believe what's back here!"

"Is it a Charizard?" Sarah asked.

"Even better!" Skip cried. "Come look!"

Doubtful that anything could be better than a rare Pokémon, Sarah took one hesitant step into the old house.

Suddenly, there was a voice from just behind her. "What are you so scared of?" it asked.

Her mother.

"I know it might look—and smell—a little bit strange, but I think you and your brother are going to love it here." Mom was carrying the first of about a hundred cardboard boxes from the U-Haul. "We used to come out here every summer when I was your age. I have so many nice memories of playing along the coast and exploring these woods. Aren't the trees beautiful this time of year?"

Sarah reluctantly surveyed the bright explosions of red, yellow, and orange all around her. "Um, I guess they look okay. But the cell signal isn't strong. It'll be really hard to get mapping programs to work."

Sarah's mother narrowed her eyes. "Is this about that game again?"

"It's not just a game!" Sarah said, all but exploding. "It's Pokémon GO! It's the best way to collect and train and evolve Pokémon ever!"

Her mother sighed. "It's also the reason you kept telling me to slow down the van on the drive here," her mother said crossly. "So you could reach those . . . What were they called?"

"PokéStops!" Sarah said. "They're so important. There where you get new Poké Balls and eggs and all sorts of things!"

Her mother set down the heavy box. It tinkled as it touched the ground. It must have been full of delicate things made of glass.

"You know, a lot of kids your age aren't even allowed to *have* their own phones yet," Mom said. "You and Skip are only eleven. You remember the rules, right?"

Sarah rolled her eyes. "Only use it for emergency calls and for Pokémon GO," she dutifully repeated.

"That's right," Mom said.

There was something Sarah had wanted to ask her mother ever since they started this move. She decided that now was the time. "Mom, why did we have to leave Chicago? All my friends were there. I know it wasn't perfect, but I liked it."

"Sometimes, people have to move," her mother said. Though the answer was short, it was spoken with affection. Mom understood that this would be a big transition.

"But why did we have to move right now?" Sarah asked. "And why did we have to come here? I've never even been to Maine."

"This is a great opportunity for us to start over," her mother said. "My aunt left us this house in her will. We'd never be able to afford a house this nice back in Chicago."

Sarah wrinkled her nose. She would have used a lot of words to describe the strange, musty house, but "nice" was not one them.

"And Clybourne is a lovely town," Mom continued. "There are excellent schools, natural beauty, and a nice downtown area where I can open a quilt shop."

Sarah's mother was a quilter. Her room was always full of bolts of fabric, and she owned the largest sewing machine that Sarah had ever seen. Sarah had asked her mother for a custom Pokémon quilt with Pikachu on it, but so far it hadn't materialized.

"I'm sorry you had to leave your friends behind," Mom continued. "I know moving away can be difficult. But I'm sure you'll make lots of new ones soon."

"I guess . . ." Sarah said glumly.

At that moment, Skip called again from the back of the house.

"Sarah, are you even listening? You *really* need to come and see this!"

Her mother smiled. "Why don't you go and see what's got your brother all riled up? Or, if you prefer, you can help me carry boxes."

"No, I'll see what he wants," Sarah said quickly, and ran into the strange house.

The house was full of furniture, but most of it was worn and covered in dust. There were old rugs on the floor and paintings of flowers and fruit baskets hanging on the walls. There were even old magazines and newspapers stacked on the tables. Sarah wondered how long her great-aunt had lived here and what kind of person she had been. Sarah had not met many of her distant relatives, and she'd never met her great-aunt.

Sarah found her brother at the back of the house standing in a long room with a wide window that opened out onto the sea.

Sarah and Skip looked similar, but they were not identical twins. Both had bright yellow hair. Sarah wore hers long and tied back in a ponytail, while Skip kept his short and spiked, so that it looked like the hair of his favorite Pokémon trainer. Sarah hated to admit it, but the look kind of worked—he *did* look like a Pokémon trainer.

"Check it out, sis," Skip said enthusiastically.

"Check *what* out? Can our phones get a signal back here, or what?"

"Actually, they can." Skip held up his phone. It displayed the familiar Pokémon GO screen with his avatar poised and ready to explore.

Sarah took out her own phone and brought up Pokémon GO. Sure enough, she had a signal, too. Maybe it wasn't going to be *so* bad out here in the middle of nowhere after all.

"But what I really wanted to show you was *this*," Skip said, glancing out through the window to the rocky coastline beyond.

Sarah followed his gaze.

There was a steep drop and a gravel path led down to the glistening water below. The beach was full of gray stones and did not look particularly inviting.

But Skip wasn't focused on any of that, Sarah realized. Instead, he was looking out at a small island no more than a hundred yards out from the coastline. There were lots of ugly gray islands that jutted out of the water when you got out to sea, but this island was totally different. This was an *island*-island. It was green, with plants growing all over it. And trees. So many trees, now displaying their full fall colors. Yet, even with their leaves beginning to shed, the trees created a canopy that prevented Sarah from seeing the island's center. The place seemed strange and mysterious. And adding to the mystery was a dirt footpath, just visible at the edge of the island, that led away from the water and quickly disappeared into the bushes and trees.

Then, suddenly, Sarah saw movement.

A small red shape flickered along the edge of the tree line. What could it be? Was it a fox? A dog? Whatever it was, it was appeared supernaturally quick. As soon as Sarah focused on the strange shape, it disappeared back into the woods.

"Wow!" was all that Sarah could think to say.

"I know, right?" Skip added cheerfully, using his free hand to slick back his spiky yellow hair. "That place looks awesome. We have to go explore it!"

"Do you think we're allowed?" Sarah asked. Sarah had recently been pushing their mother to let them make more of their own decisions. While Mom still required that they ask permission for virtually everything, Sarah was occasionally allowed to do things that Skip was not. To Sarah, this felt like progress.

"Well, *someone* has been out there," Skip said. "Just look at that path!"

"Yeah, I noticed," Sarah replied. "Could there be a boat around here? Maybe in the garage? Maybe down by the water?"

"I'll swim if I have to," Skip said. "It doesn't look that far."

Sarah didn't think that would be a good idea. Skip's heart was always in the right place, but he sometimes acted impulsively. Sarah understood that in exchange for giving her a little more freedom, her mom expected her to keep Skip from getting into too much trouble. Sarah shuddered when she imagined the mayhem Skip might cause if she weren't around. "Uh, let's look for a boat before we jump in the water," Sarah said.

Skip didn't respond. He was looking down at his phone. "You're not going to believe it . . . but this just got better!"

"How do you mean?" Sarah asked suspiciously.

"There's a PokéStop out on the island!" Skip held up his phone so that she could see. Sarah leaned in close, half-expecting some kind of prank. (Skip was always playing jokes. Most of them—in her opinion—weren't very funny.)

Sure enough, out on the island, in what must have been the center of its mysterious tree-shrouded folds, was the icon for a square, blue PokéStop. Sarah brought the map up on her own phone just to be sure. But there it was—a PokéStop out on the island.

"What, don't you trust me?" Skip said with a laugh, as he put his own phone back into his pocket.

Um, of course *I don't trust you, because you're always playing stupid jokes*, Sarah thought.

The PokéStop made Sarah even more curious about the island. Generally, you found PokéStops near interesting or important landmarks in the real world. She'd found them in town squares, next to statues and moments, and even at the entrances of stores and restaurants she liked. They tended to *correspond* to something. But, Sarah wondered, what could be important or interesting out there, on a tiny island off the coast of Maine in the middle of nowhere?

Sarah did not have time to think about these questions any further, since her mother walked into the room and set down another cardboard box with a muffled *thud*. Sarah jumped.

"The view from here is spectacular, huh?" Mom said. "I remember being a little girl and standing just where you two are standing, looking out the same window at the island for the first time. I think I might make this my quilting room. It could be a little tight fitting all my fabric samples inside, but I bet I can make it work."

"Mom, you've been out to the island?" Sarah asked. "Like, actually been there?"

To her surprise and annoyance, Sarah realized her mother had started giggling. "Of course I have, silly pants," her mother said. "The island is one of the best parts of living here. When I was your age, we used to row out to it almost every day."

"Then we *can* go out there!" Sarah exclaimed.

"Yessss," cried Skip, "where's the boat?"

"No so fast!" Mom warned. "I think the island is for *after* we're all moved in."

"But, *Mom*!" Sarah and Skip objected at the same time.

"But, what?"

Sarah paused, her mouth hanging open. For a moment, she couldn't think of what so say. "But . . . we really want to row out there."

Her mother laughed again.

"You'll go to the island, but after we finish unloading the moving fan. There are about a hundred more boxes where this came from."

"But . . ." Sarah said, looking longing out the window once more.

"No more *buts*," her mother said. "Less chatting. More moving boxes. You, too, Skip. If we get started now, we'll have everything inside the house in time for dinner."

With that, Mom turned and walked out of the room. Skip followed after her. Sarah hesitated, pausing for one last look out the window at the beckoning island beyond. There was another sudden flash of red at the foot of one of the trees—there, then gone.

Sarah turned and hurried after her mother.

Later that evening, Sarah and Skip sat at the round wooden table in their new kitchen while their mother cooked soup on the stove. Moving the boxes into the house had been tiring enough, but Sarah had insisted on opening them until she found the one containing her stuffed Squirtle, Winston. It had taken several tries, but now the Squirtle—which was half as big as her—sat on Sarah's lap while she waited for dinner.

"No Pokémon at the table," Mom called from the stove. "You know that's the rule."

"Not even Winston?" Sarah asked.

"Not even him. You can play with him after we eat."

Sarah reluctantly moved Winston to the nearest stack of cardboard boxes and carefully set him on top of it. As much as he liked Pokémon, Skip had no stuffed creatures of his own. Around a year ago, he had declared that he was, once and for all, "too old" for stuffed animals. Sarah thought he was completely crazy.

As she took her place back at the table and her mother began serving the soup, Sarah thought again of what she had seen earlier in the day.

"Mom, what lives on the island?" she asked.

Her mother cocked her head to the side. "Lives on it?"

"Yeah," said Sarah. "Like, I wonder—"

"Young lady, in this house, we say *yes*," her mother reminded her.

"I mean . . . yes," Sarah tried again (after a very discreet roll of her eyes). "Like, I wonder what kind of animals live out there? What kind of small, quick, red animals . . . ?"

"That's awfully specific," her mother observed, ladling a heaping serving of soup into her daughter's bowl. "What did you have in mind?"

"I don't know," Sarah replied honestly. "I just get the feeling that whatever lives there might be small and quick and red."

Her mother shrugged, then served herself and took a seat. "It's been years since I was out to the island. We spent so many wonderful days out there, fishing, exploring, doing *all sorts* of neat things."

"Yes, but what about the *animals*?" Sarah pressed.

Her mother smiled. "Oh, let's see. There were a few, as I seem to recall. Mostly birds. Eagles. Owls. Tiny sparrows."

"Those don't count," Skip suddenly piped up. "They're birds. They don't *just* live on the island. They fly around everywhere."

"Yeah," said Sarah. "I mean, yes. Yes. What about animals that walk on the ground?"

"Oh, well," her mother said, thinking for a moment. "Around here there are turkeys, raccoons, possums—all kinds of creatures walk on the ground. We're far enough north that you can sometimes even see a moose. There wouldn't be a moose on that island though."

"Why not?" asked Sarah.

"It's just not big enough," her mother answered. "The island, I mean. Not the moose. A moose wouldn't be able to find enough food to eat on an island so small. In just a few months it would eat all the grass and strip all the trees."

Sarah frowned. None of the creatures her mother had named sounded like the thing she'd seen.

"What else is on the island?" Skip asked.

"I don't remember anything else," their mother said. "Of course, I was there a long time ago."

"Could people have built something out there?" Skip pressed. "Something important enough that the island would have its own PokéStop?"

"If they did, I'm sure you'll find it. There's no keeping you from a PokéStop location. Just promise me that you'll always ask permission before you go out to the island. And you'll never go out there alone."

"I promise," Skip said.

Their mother turned to Sarah. "Oh yeah," she said. "I mean, oh yes. I promise, too."

"Good," Mom said. "Then we can go and see if there's still a boat down there first thing in the morning."

"In the morning?" cried Skip. "That's *hours* away."

"It's already getting dark," Mom pointed out. "You can't go at night. Would you want to be out in those trees with just a flashlight? It could get awfully scary."

Skip's face fell. It was clear from his expression that he hadn't thought of this.

"Besides, we need to get your PJ's unpacked, or were you planning on sleeping in your clothes?"

"I guess I can wait until tomorrow," Skip said reluctantly.

A few hours later, Sarah nestled in bed next to Winston the Squirtle. One good thing about the move—perhaps the *only* good thing, as far as Sarah was concerned—was that she and her brother would now have separate bedrooms. Sarah's new bedroom was on the second floor, just down the hall from Skip's. Not only was it larger than the old room they'd shared back in Chicago, but it had a bigger bed. Both she and Winston could easily fit.

"This was one of the guest rooms," her mother explained as she tucked Sarah in.

"What's a guest room?" Sarah asked.

"Some people have so many rooms in their houses, that they set one aside just in case people come to visit."

"Like a hotel room, but in your house?" Sarah asked.

"Sort of," her mother said, wrinkling her nose. "How do you like it here?"

Sarah was unsure how to answer. "Well, I like having my own room. That part is good."

"I think you'll find out that there are a bunch of things you like about Maine, once you get to exploring," her mother assured her. "My aunt was always telling me there were kids your age in this neighborhood, too. Maybe tomorrow you can go meet some of them."

"*And* explore the island," Sarah reminded her mother.

"All in good time," Mom said, turning off the light.

"Mom, just one more question before you go," Sarah called from her bed.

"What is it?" her mother asked, leaning against the doorway.

"Does it have a name?"

"Of course it does. Winston. You named it yourself."

"Not my Squirtle, silly," said Sarah. "The island. I thought islands were supposed to have names. Like Treasure Island. Or the Island of Misfit Toys."

Her mother rubbed her chin, and rolled her eyes to the ceiling. Sarah knew that this was her mother's traditional thinking expression. At least she was taking the question seriously.

"Hmm, that's funny" Mom said. "The island's too small to have an *official* name, of course, like on a map. But when I was here as a girl, there *was* a name that the local people used to call it. I think it was 'Ghost Island'."

"'Ghost Island?'" said Sarah. "Why'd they call it *that*?"

"It wasn't because it was scary or had ghosts. At least, not that I ever saw. I always found it to be the opposite of scary. It was sunny and pleasant most of the time. Who knows why the locals called it that? Country people get crazy ideas in their heads, sometimes."

"I guess so," said Sarah uneasily.

"All right," Mom said. "No more stalling. Time to go to sleep." She drew the door closed until the latch clicked.

Sarah was usually able to fall asleep quickly, but she worried it might take longer than usual. She breathed in the strange new smells of her new room and listened to the strange sounds. Or, more accurately, the *lack* of sound. In Chicago, even late at night, there was always something: cars honking, people talking out on the street, the elevated trains whooshing past on their tracks. Here in Clybourne, Maine, it was a whole lot quieter. The night was full of the sounds of insects and the very soft lapping of the water against the shore.

Even though it was different, it was also exciting. Sarah couldn't wait to explore this new habitat bright and early the next morning. She gave Winston a kiss goodnight, and shut her eyes tight. Before she knew it, she was fast asleep.

The next morning, Skip woke Sarah from her sleep. This was not unusual. Back in Chicago, they had slept in bunk beds—Skip slept on the top. This meant that whenever he bounced out of bed in the morning and climbed down the creaky ladder he would, more than likely, wake her up.

Because of this, Sarah was momentarily confused when she heard the unmistakable sound of Skip's feet padding across the floor. "Sarah, wake up!" Skip said, jostling the foot of the bed. "It's gone!"

What on earth could he be talking about, Sarah wondered.

"It's gone!" Skip repeated. "Look!"

Sarah rubbed her eyes and sat up in the bed. Daylight was just beginning to stream through the windows. Skip was standing beside her, holding up his phone.

"What're you talking about, Skip?"

"The PokéStop out on the island. It's not there anymore."

Sarah lifted an eyebrow. "That can't be right."

"Check your phone. Maybe mine is broken or buggy. I hope I don't have to reinstall."

Sarah walked over to the nightstand where she'd carefully plugged her phone into its charger the evening before. She turned it on and brought up Pokémon GO.

"Hmm," she said.

"Hmm, what?" Skip said. He was hunching close, trying to get a look at her screen.

"Get away! My phone is private."

"Then tell me what you see," Skip insisted.

"I see . . ." Sarah could hardly believe it. She'd never encountered anything like this before in all her hours of playing the game. "I see . . . that you're right. It *is* gone. All the other PokéStops are where they were the day before. I can still see a gym or two in the distance, and some rustling bushes where some Pokémon are hiding. But the island is just empty."

Skip looked at his sister. "We didn't *imagine* it, did we? I mean, it wasn't just me. You saw it, too, right?"

"Of course I did. Maybe the signal is just fuzzy up here. Come on. Let's go back downstairs and try."

Standing in their mother's new quilting studio, the results were the same. No PokéStop anywhere on the island.

"Maybe all these boxes of fabric are blocking the signal somehow," Skip said.

"Maybe we should go down to the island and check in person," Sarah suggested.

Skip nodded and smiled. He clearly liked the idea.

"But we'll need to ask permission first," Sarah said.

Together, they bounded toward the big room at the top of the house that their mother had claimed as her own.

"Mom!" Sarah cried, knocking on the door. "Something exciting happened. The PokéStop out on the island disappeared. We want to go down and see if we can find it again. Can we? Can we?"

"What time is it?" her mother's voice called from the other side of the door.

"Seven-thirty," Skip shouted brightly.

They could hear their mom mumbling.

"What did you say?" asked Sarah.

The door abruptly opened. Their mother stood in her bathrobe, looking not quite awake. The seriousness of this situation seemed, somehow, to escape her.

"A PokéStop just disappeared," Sarah explained. "This has never happened to either of us before."

"I heard you the first time," her mother said with a yawn. "All right. I suppose unpacking can wait. Let's go have breakfast. If you eat everything you're supposed to, *then* we can go find the missing PokéStop."

Sarah and Skip took off for the kitchen and found spoons, cereal bowls, and even some cereal to go inside them. One quick breakfast and change of clothes later, they were urging their mother out the back door. It opened out onto the rocky path that led down to the shore below.

"Hang on," their mother cried. "I'm still on my first cup of coffee!"

There was no handrail on the path and the rocks were sometimes loose underfoot. Despite this, Skip kept his face buried in the bright light of his phone. His spiky Pokémon trainer hair sparkled in the morning sunlight. "This way!" he called. "I can already see some Magikarp down by the waterline. Still no sign of the PokéStop, though."

No sooner were these words out of his mouth than Skip stumbled on the steep path and almost lost his footing. Sarah was quick to reach out and steady him, but her mother was quicker. She grabbed her son by the shoulder with one hand, and took his phone with the other.

"No phones if you don't have the sense to look where you're going," she said sternly.

"But *Mom*!" Skip protested.

She closed Pokémon GO and pocketed the phone, then turned to her daughter and held out her hand.

"Mom, I wasn't playing," Sarah said. "I was looking where I was going."

"Fine. But if you turn that phone on before we get down to the beach, it's going in my pocket, too."

Sarah smiled triumphantly. Skip stuck out his tongue at her, and she fought the urge to return the gesture.

"Why are you acting like such a brat, Skip?" Sarah whispered as their mother moved a few paces ahead.

"You're just jealous because I'm going to turn every gym along this whole coast yellow," Skip replied confidently.

"I will *never* understand why you chose Team Instinct," Sarah said, rolling her eyes. "Is it just because you have the same haircut as Spark? Because I don't think that's a particularly good reason to pick a team."

"You're not any better. I mean, what's so special about Team Mystic? *Everybody* chooses Team Mystic."

"That's because it's the best team!" Sarah said, her frustration growing.

"Now, Team Instinct on the other hand?" Skip continued. "It takes a special person to choose Team Instinct. An original thinker."

"What would *you* know about being an original thinker?" said Sarah.

Skip stuck out his tongue again.

A few minutes later, they reached the end of the path and were standing on the rocky beach. Mom gave Skip his phone back and he quickly turned it on and loaded up Pokémon GO.

The island was now much closer. However, this only made it even clearer to Sarah that it was too far for anyone to swim out to. You'd really need a boat.

As if reading Sarah's thoughts, her mother said, "When I was a kid, we used to keep an old wooden rowboat tied up down here, just for getting out to the island. I don't see it, but let's take a look. Maybe it's still around."

They began to explore the rocky coast. They were hit with an icy spray as the wind whipped up. The ocean smell was powerful. To Sarah, it seemed like a combination of salt water, fish that had gone bad, and some other, undefinable ingredient. The ground beneath their feet was uneven, full of pointy rocks. *It's almost as treacherous as the trail*, Sarah thought.

As they searched the shore, Skip used the opportunity to catch a couple of Magikarp, which had spawned nearby. He captured each one effortlessly with a perfect cast of his Poké Ball.

"Nice work," Sarah said.

Skip shrugged, as if to say the low-CP fish were hardly worth the effort.

Sarah began to climb a grassy hill at the edge of the beach. A few steps up, her foot unexpectedly sank through the ground. She jumped back and pulled her foot away. Then, even more unexpectedly, a family of rabbits emerge from the hole and scampered up the hill.

"Are you okay, sis?" Skip asked with genuine concern. He could be a jerk, but there was evidence that deep down he actually did care about his sister.

"I'm fine," Sarah said. "Just surprised."

A moment later, their mother arrived. "Hey, good job!" she said.

Sarah didn't understand.

"It looks like you found the boat!" Mom clarified.

Sarah looked again at the hilly lump of grass, which now had a foot-sized hole in it. "*That's* the boat?"

"What's left of it. It looks like nobody used it for so long that it got old and rotted, and grass grew on it."

"Is that *really* a boat?" Skip asked, looking skeptically at the grassy mound.

"Here, let's turn it over and I'll show you," Mom said. "Help me out."

The three of them cleared away the grass at the edge until—sure enough—an old wooden plank was revealed. They pulled on it until the hill itself began to move. There was a ripping sound as years of accumulated soil fell away. The hill began to turn, and eventually, it flipped over. Underneath was a wooden hull, three rotted seats, and a couple of worm-eaten sticks that once might have been oars.

"See?" their mother said, breathing hard from the exertion.

"Wow," Skip said quietly. "It *is* a boat. Or *was*."

Sarah frowned. "Does this mean there's no way to get out to the island?" she asked.

"It sure looks that way, kiddo. There's a loft up above the garage I haven't explored yet. I suppose there *could* be a kayak up there, or something. I really don't know."

"How are we going to get to the island then?" Sarah pressed.

"Well, we can always get a new boat somewhere in town. But that will take money. Which will mean me selling quilts. Which will mean me stitching quilts. Which will mean me getting to work, and not spending time exploring the coast."

Skip looked at his sister, then at the island beckoning across the glistening water, and then back up at his mother.

"Mom," he said seriously, "I think you should go sew some quilts."

His mother laughed. "I'm glad you agree. In the meantime, why don't you two keep each other company and try not to get in too much trouble? Sound good?"

Sarah and Skip both nodded.

"Good," their mother said. "And I think you *might* even be able to make some new friends."

"Do you mean next week, when we have to start school?" Sarah asked.

"No, I was actually thinking more of that group of kids about your age, walking down the beach right over there."

Sarah and Skip both swiveled their heads. Their mother was taller and kind of standing higher up the hill, so it took them a few moments to see, but she wasn't lying. Far down the coastline, walking toward Sarah and Skip, was a group of four kids. It looked like two boys and two girls, maybe between ten and twelve years old. They appeared to be gazing down at their phones and occasionally pausing to flick at the screens in a way that felt *very* familiar to Sarah and Skip.

"They're playing Pokémon GO, too" Sarah shouted with glee.

"Great," their mother said. "Then you'll have something in common. Now I'm going to head back up to the house to get started on my quilting. And have another cup of coffee." And with that, she stalked back up the rocky path toward the house.

"I'm so excited to meet some other kids," said Sarah. "Do you think they'll go to our school, Skip? Skip?"

He didn't respond. He was examining his hair-spikes in the reflection of a puddle. When he saw a spike that drooped, he spat on his finger and ran in through his hair to make it pointy again.

"Eww," said Sarah. "You're gross. And don't think I can't tell what you're up to. You just want to impress those new kids."

"Seeing as we're the ones who just moved here, I think *we're* the new kids, technically."

Sarah had to admit that he was right.

When all of Skip's spikes were in place, they headed toward the approaching group. Sarah was a little nervous to see the new faces, but mostly they looked friendly. And they were also into Pokémon GO. That seemed like two positive things right there. Sarah decided to hope for the best.

As they got closer, she found that their voices carried on the wind, and she could hear what they were saying.

"It's supposed to be right here," one of them insisted.

"I'm still not seeing anything," said another. "Are you *sure* this is the right location?"

"Of course I'm sure," another replied. "Did you think I was lying?"

"Hang on. Who are *those* guys? Anybody seen them before?"

Suddenly, Sarah realized she and Skip were now the topic of conversation.

The group of kids was now only a few paces away. Sarah waved at them and hoped she looked friendly.

"Hi there," Sarah said.

"Hello," one of the kids replied cautiously. He was kind of short and grumpy, but still seemed as if he might be the leader of the group. Or like he *wanted* to be the leader, at any rate.

"Are you playing Pokémon GO?" Sarah asked. "We like to play, too."

"Oh yeah," said the kid. "What level are you?"

This was, of course, a sensitive question. It separated the real Pokémon GO players from the kids who just dabbled to kill the time.

"Well . . . what level are *you*?" she replied coolly.

The short kid hesitated for a moment. He pulled his phone's screen closer to his chest, so that Sarah would not be able to get a look.

Suddenly, another girl stepped forward from the back of the group. She had dark eyes and dark hair that was spiked up a little bit like Skip's. "I'm sorry that my friend is being so rude," the girl said, putting away her phone and extending her hand. "My name's Charlotte. These two are Sammy and Maria. And this guy who doesn't want to tell you he's only Level Eighteen is my neighbor, Richard."

"Hey!" said Richard. "What gives? That's not even right. I totally leveled up again last night when you weren't around."

"I'm sure you did," said Charlotte, giving Sarah a sideways glance.

"Nice to meet you," said Sarah. "This is my brother, Skip. I'm Sarah. We just moved here from Chicago."

Richard's eyes began to twitch back and forth as though something important had been revealed.

"Which house did you move into?" he asked aggressively.

Sarah pointed back up the hill. "It's . . . I don't know what to call it. I don't even know our street address yet. It's just down the beach there. That house"

"Is it the house with the long path behind it?" Richard pressed. "The path that leads down to the water? And there's an island in the water?"

Skip and Sarah exchanged an uneasy glance.

"That's the one," Skip said. "Why are you so interested in where we live?"

"Charlotte says she's seen some strange things on that island," Richard explained. "Strange *Pokémon* things. The only problem is . . . she's lying."

"I'm *not* lying," Charlotte countered, stamping her foot into the rocky ground. "I did see those things."

"What did you see?" Sarah asked cautiously.

Charlotte hesitated.

"It's all right," Sarah added. "You can tell us. We know Pokémon GO."

Charlotte swallowed hard.

"Well, I was down here by myself the other day," Charlotte said. "I was picking up Magikarp—I'm trying to evolve a Gyarados. I wasn't paying attention to how far I'd walked, and suddenly I was standing in front of the island by your house. I took a look at my phone and it showed there was a PokéStop out on the island. There was also a Pokémon I'd never seen before. It was small and red. It sort of looked like a Charmander or maybe a Charmeleon. Or maybe even a Growlithe."

"So what happened?" Sarah asked. "Was it close enough that you could catch it?"

Charlotte nodded.

"Yes. Once I got over the initial surprise, I started tapping my screen like crazy to catch it. But then . . . then . . ." Charlotte looked crestfallen.

"What?" Sarah asked enthusiastically. "What happened."

"*My phone went dead!*" Charlotte said. "I had forgotten to charge it the night before, and right at that moment, I ran out of juice. I went straight home and recharged it, but when I came back later in the day, both the Pokémon and the PokéStop were gone!"

Richard quickly added: "That's what she *says*, anyway."

"Stop it, Richard," Charlotte cried.

"Charlotte can be kind of dramatic," Richard said.

"I'm not being dramatic," she objected. "I'm telling the truth. I really saw it." Her face began to grow red from frustration or anger or embarrassment, or possibly a combination of all three. For a moment, it seemed she might even burst into tears.

"*I* believe you," Sarah said confidently, putting her hand on Charlotte's shoulder.

"You *do?*" Charlotte said, wiping her eye.

Sarah nodded. "Because I think I've seen it, too. When we arrived at the house last night, there was a PokéStop on the island. Then it was gone. Skip also saw it. We couldn't figure out what was going on."

"I have some theories," Skip said in a confident tone he hoped made him seem like an expert Pokémon trainer.

"You do?" Sarah said doubtfully. "You haven't shared them with *me*."

Skip ignored his sister and continued. "The creators are always saying they're going to introduce new elements to the game," said Skip. "Maybe some of the new elements are PokéStops that appear and disappear, or entirely new Pokémon. Maybe the island behind our house has been selected as the first place they appear."

"Why would you put exciting new game elements on a tiny island in the middle of nowhere?" Sarah asked.

"I dunno," Skip said with a shrug. "I'm sure they have good reasons."

Richard said, "Charlotte was taking us back to the island to show us. But I can already see it in the distance on my phone, and there's no PokéStop anywhere near here."

"Why don't we come with you," Sarah suggested. "I have a feeling that something funny is going on. Let's investigate together!"

"That sounds good to me," Charlotte said with a smile.

The group headed back up the beach.

The island slowly grew closer. Sarah went back and forth between looking at the island on her phone, and looking at it directly. There was still no sign of any PokéStops or new Pokémon. Sarah and Charlotte took the lead. Behind them, Skip and Richard compared Pokémon they had caught on their phones, and Sammy and Maria quietly brought up the rear.

"Can I ask you a question?" Charlotte asked. "One that's *not* about Pokémon?"

"Sure," Sarah answered.

"Why does your voice sound like that?" Charlotte asked.

Sarah thought for a moment. "Oh," she said. "It's a Chicago accent. It's just how people talk there. Why does *your* voice sound the way *it* does?"

"It's a Maine accent," Charlotte said. "It's just how people talk *here*."

They reached the edge of the water nearest to the island, not far from where Sarah had stumbled on the overturned boat.

"Here we are," Sarah announced.

"Yes," Charlotte said. "This is *exactly* where I was when I saw it . . . and when my phone went dead."

"Everybody look around carefully," Skip said. "We're bound to find something."

Richard made a noise that sounded like *humph*. Clearly, he was still skeptical about Charlotte's claim.

All six of them took out their phones and began to survey the area. There was a rustling in the virtual grass along the inland coast, but it turned out to be a Pidgey. Sarah snapped it up quickly with a single cast of her Poké Ball.

After they had spent a solid five minutes looking around, Richard was ready to declare victory.

"See, there's nothing here," he said. "I *told* you Charlotte was being dramatic."

"But I saw it, too," Sarah reminded him. "And so did Skip."

"Then maybe all three of you are being dramatic," Richard said, sulkily. "

"What about getting out to the island?" Charlotte asked, ignoring Richard and turning to Sarah. "Some Pokémon only pop up when you're practically right on top of them. Maybe something is there, but it's hiding until we get closer."

"There used to be a boat here years ago, but now it's all rotted and rabbits live in it," Skip said, pointing to the ancient, overturned vessel.

"I could totally swim to the island if I wanted to," boasted Richard. "I just don't *feel* like it."

"I could totally swim to the island, too," added Skip.

"Nobody's swimming to the island," Sarah said firmly. "It's not safe."

"But just so you know, I could," Skip replied.

"Uhuh," Charlotte said skeptically.

"Well, there's no use standing here," Richard said. "I'm going back to my neighborhood, where there are actual, real, existing PokéStops. C'mon guys."

Richard headed down the beach, away from the island. Sammy and Maria followed him. Charlotte hesitated.

"I kind of have to go with them," she said to Sarah. "Our parents made us promise that we would stick together."

"That's okay," said Sarah. "Maybe we'll see each other again."

"Sure thing," said Charlotte. "I live in the development just a little way down the coast, and a few blocks inland. Right by the retirement home. You can't miss it."

"Cool," said Sarah. "And maybe I'll see you in school next week."

"Oh yeah," said Charlotte, her face falling a bit. "School. I keep forgetting summer vacation is almost over."

"Yeah, me, too," Sarah confessed.

"Oh well, I should go," Charlotte said, and began to plod down the shoreline after Richard and the others.

Suddenly she stopped and called back over her shoulder.

"Oh, there's one more thing I forgot to mention."

"What's that?" said Sarah.

"My family has a boat."

Sarah and Skip spent the rest of the morning exploring the coastline. There were some interesting rocks and Skip almost caught a frog, but otherwise they found nothing all that special. They walked back up to the house for lunch. Over peanut butter sandwiches, Skip and Sarah informed their mother of their encounter with the neighborhood kids.

"They sound like they're going to be nice people," Mom pronounced.

"Maybe," Skip replied. "Richard thinks he's quite a Pokémon trainer, but the Pokémon he's caught aren't really top tier. He didn't even want to tell us what level he was."

"That girl, Charlotte, sounds nice," Mom said.

"Yes, she is," said Sarah brightly between bites of sandwich. "I really liked her a lot. And, get this, she said her family has a—"

Skip swiftly kicked Sarah under the table.

"Ow!" Sarah said. "What'd you do that for?"

"We still want Mom to get us a boat of our own," Skip whispered. "She won't if she thinks we already have one."

Sarah rolled her eyes.

"At least you'll already know some of the local kids when you start school," Mom said. "Did you ask if they go to Greenleaf Middle School on Fourth Street? That's where you're registered."

"Um, we didn't ask," Sarah replied.

After lunch, Sarah and Skip helped their mother unpack more cardboard boxes. Sarah filled her new closet with clothes and decorated the walls of her room with posters—most of them related to Pokémon. She got tired before she could finish the job. There was nothing like moving all your stuff to make you appreciate how much stuff you had!

Sarah decided to lie down on her bed and take a short nap. She'd earned it. Whether it was the excitement of meeting new friends or the exhaustion that came from opening box after box after box of clothes and toys, Sarah found herself slipping into dreamland deeper than she'd intended to.

All at once, she was in a forest place. A clearing nestled in the center of rows of maple and birch trees. In the dream, it wasn't early fall, but late spring. The leaves on the trees were healthy and green. The sun above sparkled through them creating a shimmering chandelier effect. Out of the corner of her eye, she caught a flash of orange-red that didn't come from any tree. Sarah turned to look and saw a two-foot lizard standing beside a thick maple. It had big expressive eyes and a friendly mouth with only four teeth. Its skin was dark orange. Its long tail flopped back and forth behind it like a snake.

At the tip of the tail, a small flamed glowed, no larger than a lit match. Yet something told Sarah that this flame could easily become much, much larger with a change in the creature's disposition.

"Wow, a Charmander," Sarah said to herself.

The Pokémon did not confirm or deny this, but only smiled up at Sarah.

"What do you want, little guy?" Sarah asked.

She was about to add another question—"Where are we?"—but she already knew the answer. Even thought she'd never been there before in waking life, she was certain she was on the island behind her house. There was no other place that this could be.

The Charmander turned and ran into the trees. Sarah watched as its fiery tail flickered out of sight. She wondered where it was hurrying off to. (She also wondered how Charmanders didn't cause forest fires wherever they went.)

"Hey," she called. "Wait up! Where are you going?"

Sarah sprinted into the trees after the tiny animal. For a lizard, it could move pretty quickly! She lost sight of the creature in the maze of branches a couple of times, but she always figured out which way it had gone.

After several minutes of chasing the Pokémon, Sarah caught up. The Charmander had had led her to another clearing deep in the trees, and taken a seat on the grass. It was looking away from Sarah, up at something high in the sky above. Sarah slowed her pace and crept closer.

"Hello?" she called. "Charmander? Hello?"

The Charmander looked back in her direction once, then turned its enormous eyes skyward again. Sarah stepped out of the trees and into the clearing. All at once, she realized what had captivated the Charmander.

There, rotating high in the sky above the island was what could only be a Pokémon gym. It was composed of three enormous metallic discs that floated, one atop the other. The two lower discs were small, but the disc on top was huge. Large enough for several Pokémon to fight on top of it. Which was exactly what appeared to be happening at the moment.

As Sarah and the Charmander looked on, a Magmar launched flame at a Poliwrath. As the Poliwrath fell, a Sandslash rose to take its place. The spiky, clawed Pokémon used its enormous talons to shake the floor of the disc that held the Magmar, sending it careening all around the gym.

The action was exciting, and for a moment Sarah was completely caught up in the contest. But after a few moments, it struck her that something was not quite right here. The colors of the gym were wrong. Certainly, there was the blue of Team Mystic, the red of Team Valor, and the yellow of Team Instinct. But there also seemed to be *other* colors represented. Colors that Sarah had never before seen in any game of Pokémon. Were those orange, purple, and black teams playing? Sarah squinted, trying to figure out if her eyes were playing tricks on her. She had no other explanation. But how could that be? Everyone knew, there were only three teams.

"Charmander," she said. "What is this? Why are you showing me this?"

The Charmander turned to face her. It opened its wide, friendly mouth.

And Skip's voice came out.

"Who are you calling a Charmander?"

Sarah started awaken. She sat up in her bed and rubbed her eyes. Skip stood at the doorway to her room, an amused look on his face.

"I didn't . . ." Sarah sputtered, trying to explain herself. "I mean . . ."

"I am *so* glad we don't have to share a bedroom anymore," Skip said. "Because you are *totally* weird."

"Whatever," said Sarah, rising to her feet. "I was just having a dream. What do you want?"

"Mom said I should come get you," Skip said, before heading back downstairs.

Sarah took a deep breath and tried to remember details of the dream. It was very strange. Maybe it had been brought on by something she'd eaten. Somewhere, Sarah had heard that certain foods could cause odd dreams. Maybe the peanut butter sandwiches from lunch were not agreeing with her.

Then her mother's voice came from the bottom of the staircase: "Sarah, are you awake?"

Giving the dream no further thought, Sarah closed the door behind her and walked downstairs.

They went shopping. Mom bought Sarah and Skip school supplies, and also took them to a grocery store to stock up on supplies. Downtown Clybourne was nothing like downtown Chicago. But this was not an entirely bad thing, Sarah decided. The people they talked to seemed friendly and there were plenty of places to park their car. Even more unbelievably, the parking meters only cost a dime.

Mom pulled up beside a tiny, dark storefront along Clybourne's main street. "That's where

I'm going to have my quilt store," she told them. "I've already signed the lease. What do you kids think?"

"I like it," said Sarah. "It's a very good location."

"I like that there's an ice cream store two doors down," said Skip. He had a thing for ice cream.

The car filled with groceries and school supplies, they drove back home. Sarah and Skip broke out their phones and played Pokémon GO along the way. Yet there were few PokéStops on this part of the journey, and Sarah only caught a couple of Weedles. Catching the Weedles also required more casts of her Poké Ball than usual. Something was bothering Sarah. She couldn't get the strange Charmander dream out of her mind.

When they arrived at the house, Sarah helped her mother carry the groceries inside.

"How are you liking Maine so far?" Mom asked.

"It good," Sarah said.

"Just good?"

"I like having my own room. I also like the kids we met."

"That's nice to hear," her mother said.

Suddenly, Skip appeared holding a basketball.

"What are you doing with *that*?" Sarah asked. "You know I hate basketball."

Sarah liked lots of different sports, but basketball had never caught on with her. Skip, on the other hand, was crazy about it and played all the time. Almost as much as he played Pokémon GO.

"This isn't for you," Skip said. "I'm going to practice my dribbling in the driveway."

"Fine," Sarah said. "Have fun."

"I *will*," said Skip. "While I'm playing the *best sport ever.*"

"You're crazy," Sarah said as he stalked out of the kitchen.

"Basketball rules!" Skip called back.

Sarah heard the front door close behind him.

"So what are you going to do while Skip plays basketball?" Mom asked. "Do you want to help me put away groceries and sort fabric samples?"

Sarah was already thinking about her dream again. And she didn't want to sort fabrics.

"Um, I was actually thinking I might go for a walk. Do a little more exploring."

"Where?" her mother asked cautiously.

"Down by the water," Sarah answered.

"Yes . . . Let's make it a rule that you and Skip need to stick together when you go down there. It can be dangerous around water, and that path is pretty steep."

"But *Mom*!"

"Look, we both know you're more responsible than Skip. And that's why I'm going to give you permission to go exploring anywhere you like. . . . Just not down by the water, okay?"

"I guess," Sarah said. Her mother's word was the law. It wasn't really like she had a choice. For the hundredth time, Sarah wished that her mother would let her make more of her own decisions.

"Good," Mom said, lifting a sack of peaches out of a grocery bag and placing them into a bowl. Have fun, and try not to get into trouble."

"Okay," Sarah said.

"And watch out for strangers and bears," her mother said. "They have those around here."

"We had strangers back in Chicago," Sarah said.

"I meant the bears, silly."

"We had those, too," Sarah replied, and headed out of the kitchen through the front hallway, and out the front door.

Skip was doing bounce passes against the side of the house.

"See ya, Skip," Sarah said.

He looked at her for a moment and grunted noncommittally. Then he went back to his bounce passes.

Sarah turned left along the gravel driveway and walked down to the road that ran away from the house. There was no sidewalk, so Sarah walked along the grassy shoulder. There were few cars and no other foot traffic. Their house was technically at the very edge of the Clybourne town limits. Sarah could tell from what she'd seen down on the beach that they had neighbors, but there were no other houses immediately in sight. Just acres and acres of tall trees and rich foliage.

Sarah took out her phone and began to play Pokémon GO as she explored. There were a couple of Caterpie nearby. She captured the cute little guys with a single cast each, and found she now had enough Caterpie candy to evolve a Metapod. She evolved it . . . and then felt instantly bad. Being a Metapod looked terribly boring to Sarah. You lost all the cute little legs and feelers you had as a Caterpie, and your body got all hard and angular. Sarah resolved to gather enough candy to evolve it to a Butterfree as soon as possible.

After ten minutes of walking, Sarah reached an intersection. In the Pokémon GO world, two PokéStops unfolded as she approached. One of them had been recently activated with a lure module. Obviously, she wasn't the only Pokémon trainer in the neighborhood. Sarah wondered if the lure might have been placed by Charlotte or another of her friends, or by another player entirely. It was exciting to think about!

Sarah swiped both PokéStops and collected several new Poké Balls, a Super Potion, and a couple of Razz Berries. The lure had summoned a Spearow and a Sandshrew. Sarah made short work of them, snapping them up with a few practiced casts. The Sandshrew kicked out of her Poké Ball a couple of times, but she eventually got it to stick. She always did.

"Stupid Sandshrew," Sarah said to herself. "Think you're too good for my collection of Pokémon? You better think again."

Now that the PokéStops were tapped out of treasure—and no other Pokémon lurked nearby— Sarah thought about her next move. If she took the left turn in the next intersection, she'd find some rustling bushes that held the promise of even more Pokémon. Her radar said an Oddish and a Tentacool were both nearby. Not top-shelf, but they would do.

Sarah took the turn at the intersection and headed down the new road. She could hear the water growing louder on the eastern side of the trees. She was more or less following along the coast, she realized. Knowing this helped her feel less disoriented and confident she'd be able to find her way home.

As she closed in on the rustling bushes, she saw the potential Pokémon were not directly along the side of the road, but set back several yards into the woods. Just as she began to wonder if it would be worth risking ticks and poison ivy to forge through the underbrush, she noticed an unexpected opening in the trees. It was an old dirt road, just wide enough for a car. Two tire ruts had been seared permanently into it.

Sarah stood at the entrance to the drive and wondered if she should keep going. The woods beyond looked dark and forbidding. Then she heard a voice.

"Oh *darn* it!"

It sounded older and female.

Sarah put her hand to her ear and listened.

There was a strange clanking sound, like metal against metal. Then the voice came again. "Come *on* now."

The voice was angry, but also playful. Clearly, its owner was frustrated by something . . . but not anything too serious. Just something annoying. It reminded Sarah of how *she* sounded when she was having trouble capturing a Pokémon, when she obviously threw the Poké Ball right where the Pokémon was standing but *somehow* it jumped or ducked at the exact same moment, and she'd just wasted an Ultra Balls! *What was up with that?*

In short, Sarah felt she could relate to this person, whatever frustration she might be feeling.

Feeling bolder, Sarah began down the dirt road. The metal clanks increased in volume. Sometimes they were followed by dull metal thuds. The grumpy voice also got louder.

Sarah checked her phone. The rustling in the virtual bushes had stopped, and a Magnemite hovered in its place.

"*Yes*," Sarah said. She had been hoping to evolve a new, higher-CP Magneton soon. This would be an excellent step on the path to doing that.

Sarah tapped on her screen and prepared to capture the Magnemite. It spawned on her screen and hovered in the air, its probing magnet arms seemingly ready for mischief. Sarah picked up her first Poké Ball and prepared to throw it. She continued walking forward. Suddenly, a voice shook her back to the real world.

"Young lady? Excuse me? Young lady?"

Sarah looked up and saw the source of the clanking sounds—and the complaining. It was an elderly woman with long silver hair. She wore a long dress and a shiny necklace. She was barefoot. In her hand was a metal horseshoe.

Sarah realized she had wandered farther than she thought while preparing to catch the

Magnemite. From this perspective, she could see not only the woman, but a seaside cottage at the edge of the cliff behind her. In the center of the lawn in front of the cottage, a short metal spike stuck up out of the ground. The bright green grass all around it was littered with horseshoes.

"Can I help you?" the elderly lady said.

"Oh, sorry," said Sarah. "I was just, uh . . ."

For about the hundredth time since she had started playing Pokémon GO, Sarah wondered how to explain it to someone who was not familiar. Some people—you could usually tell them just by look-ing—were not going to have heard of the game, and would have no idea what you were talking about.

"Let me guess," the woman said before Sarah could finish. "You got distracted playing a game."

Sarah's eyes went wide. Maybe the woman *did* understand.

"That's actually exactly what it was."

"I can relate," the woman said. "I distract myself with games all the time. Doing it at this very moment."

Sarah looked again at the horseshoes in her hands. They were old and caked with mud.

"Are you from around here?" the woman asked. "I haven't seen you before."

She turned her head slightly to the side and looked Sarah up and down.

"We just moved here," Sarah replied. "My family did, that is. My brother and my mom and me. We just arrived last night. We live in the big house just down the street."

A look of recognition spread over the woman's face. "The old Baker place?"

Sarah nodded. "Mary Baker was my mom's aunt," Sarah told the woman. "I guess that makes her my great-aunt? I never met her."

"Well, I'll tell you something," said the woman, leaning closer to Sarah. "I did meet her. I knew her well. I knew your mother too, I expect. Back when she was a girl about . . . oh . . . about your age, I should think."

Sarah could only nod. She didn't know quite what to say.

"Your name is . . . Sarah," the woman said. "And you have a brother called Skipper."

"That's right!" Sarah said. "Except my brother likes to be called Skip now. He thinks he's all adult."

It was an odd feeling to realize a strange woman knew about your family.

"Your aunt used to mention her great-niece and nephew," the woman said. "And I never forget a name. Faces are another matter, of course."

"What's *your* name?" Sarah asked. "You know who I am. I feel like I should know who you are."

"Where are my manners?" the woman said. "My name is Alice. Alice Barstow." She dropped the remaining horseshoes, wiped her hand against the side of her dress, and held it out. Sarah put her phone in her pocket and they shook hands.

"I was just playing horseshoes," Alice said. "Have you ever played?"

"No, but it's funny. You were making the same noises that I make playing Pokémon GO." Sarah expected Alice to ask for an explanation, but instead she nodded as if she understood.

"Would you like to give horseshoes a try?" Alice asked. "You don't play it on your phone, but you still might enjoy it. There's no trick to it. Which is *precisely* the trick to it."

Alice walked over to the metal stake and picked up the horseshoes surrounding it. Then she walked back over to Sarah and handed her half of the horseshoes.

"I throw them and try to hit that pole?" Sarah asked. "What's the best way to do it?"

"Oh, there are about a hundred different ways to throw a horseshoe," Alice said. "You have to pick the one that works for you. That's the challenge."

Sarah took one of the horseshoes, reared back like a baseball pitcher, and sent it flying toward the stake. It landed several feet short and a good way off to the right. "Ugh," she said. "Let me try that again."

She took another horseshoe and this time held it like a Frisbee flying disc. She jerked back her arm and flung it. The twist of metal went careening through the air. This time, it sailed over the stake entirely, landing very far away.

"You might fare better throwing underhand," Alice suggested. "Then again, you might not."

Sarah looked at the older woman doubtfully, then took a horseshoe and threw it forward from between her knees with both hands. (Sarah had, for many years, called this "throwing granny-style." In this situation, she made a point of not even thinking the words, as Alice was quite probably a granny herself, if not a *great*-granny.) The grimy metal U spun end-over-end and came to rest just in front of the metal stake.

"See, that's wasn't too bad," Alice observed.

"This is a little like throwing Poké Balls," said Sarah. She wiped a bead of sweat from her forehead. All this walking and throwing things was hot work.

"Poké Balls?" Alice asked politely. "How exotic-sounding. What are they exactly?"

"They're these balls you throw to catch Pokémon in Pokémon GO," Sarah explained. "You can throw them by flicking your finger. There are lots of ways to do it. You can throw curveballs or throw straight on or make the Poké Ball arc. The Pokémon are sometimes hard to hit. They'll jump out of the way or put up some kind of defense at the last minute. And then, even after you trap the Pokémon inside the ball, they can still pop out, and you have to capture them all over again. But that's a whole different problem."

Alice nodded seriously, as though she got the idea. "You like playing games, then?" the older lady asked.

"I never really thought about it," Sarah said. "I guess so. I sure do like playing Pokémon GO."

"Hmm, must be hereditary," Alice said with a grin. Sarah noticed that despite her age, the woman's teeth were perfectly white and polished almost to a gleam.

"What do you mean, *hereditary*?" asked Sarah.

"Oh, it's just that your mother liked games a lot when she was your age," Alice said mysteriously.

"My mother only told us a little about when she stayed here," Sarah said. "It was a long time ago. My mom's really old."

Suddenly, Sarah remembered that she was talking to someone old enough to be her mother's grandmother. "That is . . . What I meant was . . ."

Alice smiled.

"Fifteen or sixteen seems mighty old when you're just eleven," Alice said.

"How did you know I'm eleven?" Sarah asked.

Alice merely touched her nose twice with two fingers. Sarah understood that this meant it was a secret.

"But I'll tell you," Alice continued. "I'm many years away from fifteen or sixteen, but—would you believe?—there are still folks who seem awfully old to me, too."

Sarah giggled.

At that moment, Sarah's phone vibrated. She looked down to see if it was signaling another Pokémon in the vicinity. Instead, there was a text from her mother: *Pls head home. Time to wash up for dinner.*

Sarah glanced at the clock on her phone and realized it was later than she thought. "Wow," she said. "The time really slips away from you when you're catching Pokémon and meeting new people. I need to be going before I get in trouble! It was nice to meet you, Alice."

"Same here," said the woman.

Sarah turned to retrace her steps back to the main road. Before she had gotten very far, she again heard Alice's voice.

"Before you leave, tell me on thing. What has your mother told you about . . . the *island*?"

Sarah stopped dead in her tracks. "*You* know about the island?" Sarah asked.

Alice did not immediately respond.

Sarah waited for a reply, then turned back around.

But Alice was no longer there.

Sarah looked back and forth across the property, dumbfounded. The house was still there. The grounds and lawn were still there. But the woman with whom she had been speaking had somehow vanished! Sarah looked around for where she might be hiding.

"Alice?" Sarah said. Her voice had fallen to a whisper.

There was a loud clinking sound.

Sarah jumped.

Gazing in the direction of the noise, she saw that one of the metal horseshoes had fallen off of a stack and landed on the ground.

Sarah hurried home. She was so nervous, she didn't even stop to play Pokémon GO along the way.

"Hey Lickitung, pass the potatoes."

Sarah did not move.

"Sarah, your brother's talking to you," Mom said. "I think."

They sat around the dinner table, ready to enjoy their evening meal. Skip was covered in grime and sweat from playing basketball. It was clear from the way he smelled that he hadn't showered. He seemed to enjoy being disgusting. Sarah decided there was definitely something wrong with her brother.

"I'll pass him the potatoes," Sarah said. "But not when he calls me a Lickitung."

"Well, I already tried calling you a Bulbasaur and an Oddish, but you didn't react to those, either," Skip said. "You're distracted tonight, sis."

"Jokes on you, because I like Oddish. Their little smiles are cute. Bulbasaur, I could take or leave." She reluctantly passed the potatoes.

"You *do* seem different, honey," said Sarah's mother. "You haven't been yourself since you took your walk. Did something happen?"

"No," Sarah said quickly.

"Are you *sure*?" Mom pressed as she took some potatoes for herself.

"I . . . I met a weird old lady. She lives nearby. Maybe the next house down the coast."

"It couldn't have been Old Alice, could it?" her mother asked. "No. She must be long gone."

"It *was*!" Sarah said. "She said her name was Alice Baker, and that she knew you when you when you were my age, and used to come here in the summer. We played horseshoes and I told her a little about Pokémon GO."

"I can't believe it," said Sarah's mother. "Alice is still around? My goodness! I'll have to go over and catch up with her. You were playing horseshoes, you say?"

"That's right."

"That does sound like her," Mom said. "I'm sorry if she scared you. She always was a bit strange, but she's harmless, really. She just likes to play games."

"I see," said Sarah.

"Skip, how was your afternoon?" Mom asked, changing the topic.

"Awesome," said Skip. "I'm definitely going to make the team. I don't know if our new school has one, but if it does, I'm definitely going to make it. Also, do you think there's any chance we could get a basketball hoop? That would really help me practice."

"Do you want me to start saving for a basketball hoop or for a rowboat?" Mom asked. "Both are expensive."

"I dunno," said Skip. "Probably the hoop."

He looked over at Sarah with a sweaty smile, to see if she would challenge him. Yet after Alice's strange question about the island, Sarah's curiosity had mixed with anxiety. The island was even affecting her dreams. There would be plenty of time to explore in the weeks and months ahead. Besides, Charlotte had said she had a boat.

To everyone's surprise, Sarah answered, "You know . . . I think maybe we *should* get a basketball hoop instead. Skip really seems to want it."

Skip opened his mouth to object, but stopped when he realized the unthinkable had happened—his twin sister had agreed with him.

"Well then, it's settled," said their mother. "And with much less fighting than usual. Good job, you two. See how easy things go when you decide to cooperate?"

Skip smiled, clearly satisfied. Sarah decided to let him have this one. She focused on her dinner without saying a word.

Toward the end of the meal, Skip began to think victory had been a little *too* easy. Maybe Sarah was up to something.

But by then, of course, it was far too late for Skip to say anything about it.

PART TWO

The next week, fall classes began at Greenleaf Middle School. The school was close to where Sarah and Skip lived. When the weather was nice they could walk, which was always a good opportunity to catch more Pokémon.

Sarah had learned on the first day that the trek took exactly half an hour each way. This was perfect, because she could use a lure or Magic Egg without wasting any of it. (Sarah thought it was the absolute worst when you activated something, but then reached your destination before it was done! She was very practical, and always sought to get the most out of her resources.)

It turned out, not only was Charlotte in the same grade as Sarah, but they had homeroom together, and were in several of the same classes. Sarah's favorite class quickly became science. Her teacher, Mr. Davis, had big hands like a Poliwrath, but a friendly expression like a Poliwag. Sarah thought it was a good combination. She had a few classes with Skip, too, but he quickly made his own group of new friends. Most of them were boys who also played basketball. That was all right as far as Sarah was concerned. She saw enough of Skip at home.

Greenleaf also had a Pokémon gym that was *just* accessible from the edge of the playground.

Sarah had been pleased to find that the Pokémon left by other players to man it were ones she could easily defeat. Apparently, Sarah wasn't the only student who liked to stand at the edge of the playground at recess and spend time trying to take (or re-take) the gym.

With all the new faces, new classes, and new responsibilities, the mysterious island at the back of her house was pushed from Sarah's mind. For a while, at least. There was just so much to do and think about!

Then one day a couple of weeks after the start of school, Sarah was sitting with Charlotte at lunch when they had an important conversation. Out of nowhere Charlotte said, "So I just wanted to you to know something . . ."

"Yes?" asked Sarah, wondering what it could be.

"I haven't forgot about my family's boat. I think it would be perfect for going to the island behind your house. It easily seats two or three, and it's got life vests and oars and everything."

"Oh yeah!" said Sarah. "There's been so much going on since school started, I almost forgot about the mystery of the island."

"Here's the thing," said Charlotte. "I don't exactly have permission to use it . . . but I also don't *not* have permission. Do you follow?"

"Uh, not exactly," Sarah said.

Charlotte rolled her eyes. "I mean my parents haven't told me I can use it. But they also haven't told me I can't use it. It's never come up. So . . ."

"So if you just went ahead and took the boat . . ." Sarah said, catching on.

"Exactly," said Charlotte. "If they say no, it's like, 'whoops, I thought I could.' And I don't think I'll get in *big* trouble. In my house, you get in more trouble for breaking a rule you know is a rule, than for breaking one that is just, you know, *probably* a rule."

"That's a good system."

"But I'll need your help. The boat will take at least two of us to carry from my house to the water. And if my parents are around—or driving home from work, or something—and they see us with the boat . . ."

"They could say no and make us put it back in the garage?"

"We keep it in a shed in back, actually, but—bingo."

"That *does* make it harder," Sarah said. "Well . . . what if I had my mom talk to your mom and promise to be a chaperone on our trip? Maybe your parents would be okay with it then."

"I've got an even better idea," Charlotte said, tenting her fingers like a cartoon villain. "On

Saturday, my dad will be away on a business trip and my mom has her book club meeting. So I'll be . . ."

"*Home alone*!" Sarah said. That was a rare privilege, and one she had not yet been given, even with all her good behavior.

"No, no, no," said Charlotte. "Don't be crazy. They wouldn't leave me by myself for that long. But the babysitter they get, Karen? Let's just say she does *not* know what the rules are."

"So if Karen was there, and we took the boat down to the water?"

"She would say fine, and start texting her boyfriend. She pretty much lets me do whatever I want."

"Wow," said Sarah.

"So what do you think?" Charlotte said excitedly. "Do you want to do it? To go see the island?"

"Yes," said Sarah enthusiastically.

"Good, because I do, too. I'm still convinced there's a PokéStop on the island. I know what I saw, and you said you saw it, too."

"I did!" Sarah considered also telling her friend about the strange dream she had about the island and the strange flash of a quick, red animal that she had seen, but decided to keep it to herself for the moment.

"Great," said Charlotte. "We can work out the details later. There's only one more thing we should settle now."

"What's that?" asked Sarah.

"Do we tell your brother or not?"

"If Skip finds out, he'll want to come. But if he's off playing basketball, or something, then it could just be us, having an adventure on our own. He'll be jealous later when he learns we went to the island, but . . ."

"But, what?" asked Charlotte.

"But he can just deal with it!"

"Ha! That sounds good to me."

Suddenly, both their phones vibrated. They knew what that meant and looked at each other with a grin. They always left Pokémon GO turned on during lunch because recess came right after, and often they could keep an eye on any Pokémon that might be spawning on the playground.

Both girls snatched up their phones.

"It's an Abra," said Sarah.

"Awesome," replied Charlotte. "I'm gonna go catch it."

"Not if I catch it first."

The girls hurried their lunch trays to the receptacles by the trash bins and raced outside to the playground.

The rest of the week passed quickly. The lure of going to the island once again took hold in Sarah's mind. When Saturday morning finally came, she rolled out of bed feeling like a secret agent on a mission. It was exciting, but also a little nerve-wracking. As she ate her cereal, she watched Skip out of the corner of her eye. She wondered what he would to do with his day. On Sunday they both did chores, but Saturdays they usually had to themselves.

"Mom, Sarah's being weird," Skip announced from above his glass of orange juice.

"What?" Sarah said. "No, I'm not."

"She keeps looking at me funny," Skip insisted.

"No I don't, weirdo."

"Whatever," Skip said, wiping his mouth with a paper towel and pushing himself back from the table. "It's too nice outside to hang around with weirdos. I'm gonna go ride my bike around the neighborhood. Maybe I'll find an awesome Pokémon that I won't tell anybody else about, *including my twin sister.*"

"Just remember, no riding and Pokémon-ing at the same time," said their mother. "That's not safe. Now promise me. I want to hear you say it."

"Okay," Skip said defensively. "Relax. I totally promise to pull over before I look at my phone."

Skip excused himself and headed for the front yard where his bike was parked under a covered trellis beside the garage.

Sarah couldn't believe her luck.

"What about you, missy? Going to keep me company while I do some quilting. I'm working in some really exciting purples today. Of course, they don't call them purples—not if you're a real quilter. They have dramatic names like 'Summer Lilac' and 'Royal Violet.'"

"Those are some great names for colors," Sarah said, "but I have plans with Charlotte."

"Oh, the girl you told me about? She sounds nice. What are you going to do?"

"Actually, Charlotte has a boat," Sarah said. "We were going to try taking it to the island behind the house. With your permission, of course."

"Hmm," Sarah's mother said thoughtfully. "That ought to be okay. The water out to the island isn't very deep. And the sea looks calm today. But if that changes, you'll both need to come right in. And you'll both wear life vests, right? And you both know how to swim?"

"Of course," said Sarah. "We'll be just fine. And we won't be out there for long. We just want to see the island."

"I suppose that's okay, then," Sarah's mother said cautiously. "And I'll be able to watch you from the window of my quilting room. I can see all the way to the island. Okay. Go ahead."

The instant these words out of her mother's mouth, Sarah leaped down from her chair and headed out the door to Charlotte's house.

"Thanks mom!" she called behind her. "I'll be back soon . . . with Charlotte . . . and a boat!"

At Charlotte's house, Sarah waited patiently while Charlotte explained the situation to her babysitter Karen.

"So you're, like, going over to your friend's house, or something?" Karen said, chewing her gum as she sent a text.

"Yes, my parents gave me permission to do that, remember? As long as I'm back before dark?"

"Hi," Sarah said, waving. "I'm the friend."

Karen looked up at Sarah. Her expression said she saw nothing remarkable. She quickly went back to her phone. "And you want to take the boat?"

"That's right," Charlotte said.

"My mom will be watching us the whole time," Sarah added nervously. "She can see the water from the window in the room where she works. It has a big window that looks out on the sea."

"*What*ever," Karen said, smacking her gum.

Charlotte and Sarah shared an excited glance.

Then, just as swiftly, something seemed to occur to Karen. She stopped chewing her gum and looked up with a grimace on her face. Sarah and Charlotte both swallowed hard.

"But if you damage the boat, you are *so* owning up and taking the blame. Your parents are *not* gonna take that out of my pay."

Both girls breathed a secret sigh of relief.

"No worries," said Charlotte. "We'll be extra careful. We promise. Okay?"

Karen shrugged and made an expression that said, *So why are you even still here talking to me?*

Sarah and Charlotte took the cue and scurried away to the shed.

It was about a twenty-minute walk from Charlotte's house to Sarah's, but it took longer when you were wearing a life vest and carrying a heavy rowboat with the oars inside. As they walked, the oars rocked back and forth, making loud banging noises. By the time they got to Sarah's house, they were both feeling sweaty and worn out.

"I kind of hope we *do* end up capsizing in the water," Sarah said. "Taking a dip sounds really good right now."

"But then our phones might get wet, and then we wouldn't be able to see whatever's at the PokéStop," Charlotte pointed out.

"Oh," Sarah said. "I hadn't thought of that."

As they carried the boat around the side of the house they saw that Sarah's mother was there waiting for them, sitting in a lawn chair and drinking a glass of iced tea. She wore a large floppy hat to protect her face from the sun.

"There you girls are," she said pleasantly, rising to her feet.

"Mom, I thought you were going to watch us from *inside* the house," Sarah said.

Ignoring her, Mom said, "And you must be Charlotte. I've heard such nice things. I'm very pleased to meet you."

They set down the boat so that she and Charlotte could shake hands.

"I thought you girls might want some help getting down to the water. Goodness knows this path is awfully steep."

Sarah was about to object—they really didn't need any help at all, and her mother should just *go inside and do quilting*—but then she remembered how tired and sweaty she already was and how heavy the boat had started to feel. She looked into Charlotte's face and saw her friend also looked exhausted.

"Well, maybe just down the steeper parts of the path, Mom," Sarah said.

Her mother smiled and picked up the boat single-handedly. Her mother was quite strong, perhaps more so than the two girls combined. With her mom doing the lion's share of the carrying, the three carefully walked down the steep gravel path to the water.

They set down the boat and it made a strange metallic hissing sound against the rocky shore.

Sarah had not done much boating back in Chicago—except to sit in sightseeing tours along the Chicago River—but Charlotte took charge and showed her how to climb aboard properly, and how to and cast off into the water.

"Mom," Sarah said as they began to paddle away, "you're not going to stand there on the beach and watch us the whole time, are you?"

"Maybe I am," her mother said with a smile. "What're you gonna do to stop me?"

As the boat carried her farther and farther from shore, Sarah had to admit her mother had a point. Sarah's mother could do as she wished.

"Not to be rude, but can you stop looking back at your mom and help me?" Charlotte asked.

"Oh," said Sarah. "Sorry."

Sarah readied her oar and joined Charlotte in paddling toward the island.

As she worked the oar, Sarah looked down at the blue-green seawater beneath them. It didn't look very deep. She wondered what kind of fish or marine life might be swimming around, or even *beneath* them.

Sarah also thought about what Pokémon they might discover at their destination. She wanted to take out her phone that moment, but fought the urge. *Paddling first*, she told herself. *Pokémon GO second.*

They neared the island.

"Pretty soon, you'll hear the bottom of the boat scrape," Charlotte told Sarah. "Don't worry; that's normal. When it does, it means it's shallow enough for us to get out."

Sure enough, there was soon a loud *BRRAAAAAP* as the vessel came into contact with underwater rocks on the island's shore.

"This is so exciting," Sarah said as she hopped out into the water. She had rolled up her pants and was wearing flip flops. The cool water felt good on her feet.

Sarah and Charlotte pulled the boat up onto the island and put the paddles inside.

Gazing back to land, Sarah saw her mother had left the shore. For a moment this made her breathe a little easier. Then her eye caught a flicker of movement along the path down to the beach from the house. She realized her mother had only gone back to get her lawn chair, and was now bringing it back to the beach. Sarah's mother saw the girls looking and did a big wave over her head. Reluctantly, Sarah waved back.

"Don't worry," Charlotte whispered. "If you don't like being watched, remember that she won't be able to see us once we go into the trees."

"Why are you whispering?" Sarah asked. "We're like a hundred yards away from her."

Then, suddenly, she heard her mother's voice, distant but clear: "Hello girls! Have fun! Stay safe!"

"Sound can travel in strange ways over water," Charlotte said. "You never can tell when someone is going to be able to hear you. Or you're going to hear them."

The girls turned on their phones.

"This is the moment of truth," said Sarah as the familiar loading screen blinked awake.

"I kind of don't want to say anything," Charlotte said. "I'm afraid I'll jinx it. Not like we'll *catch* a Jinx, but . . . you know what I mean."

Both girls held their breaths as their avatars loaded.

At first glance, the virtual version of the island appeared empty. No Pokémon. No PokéStops. And, most certainly, no gyms.

"Oh drat," Sarah said. "We came all this way for nothing."

"Wait a minute," Charlotte said, rotating the radar on her phone. "I'm seeing a rustling in the bushes just a few paces in. Take a look."

Sarah surveyed her own phone. Now that she looked more closely, there did seem to be a rustling in the virtual greenery toward the island's center—a telltale sign that at least one Pokémon was there to be caught.

"I see it, too," Sarah said. "C'mon, let's go see what it is!"

They crossed the rocky beach and made their way over to the worn dirt path into the trees. It looked like it had not been used in some time. Then again, a good solid thunderstorm would be enough to wash away any recent footprints, and it had rained earlier in the week.

Once they'd passed the tree line, it was suddenly much darker. Sarah though this was a benefit—it was now much easier to see details on her phone. But, it was also just a little bit scary.

"Did you hear that?" Charlotte asked.

"What?" said Sarah. "I didn't hear anything. Is your phone signaling that there are Pokémon around?"

Charlotte shook her head. "I don't mean the soundtrack on the game," she said. "I mean around us. It just got really quiet. Did you notice it, too?"

Sarah hadn't . . . but now that Charlotte mentioned it, the trees surrounding them *did* seem to have had a strange muffling effect. Sarah closed her eyes and listened. She couldn't hear the crashing of the waves out on the rocky beach. She couldn't hear the birds chirping in the trees around her. All she took in was her own breathing and Charlotte's tentative footfalls nearby.

"I see what you mean," Sarah said. "It's kind of eerie."

Charlotte nodded but said nothing else. They continued in the direction of the rustling bushes. Sarah was acutely aware of her surroundings. As they walked, she actually spent more time looking at the scenery than she did looking at her screen. She wondered about the island, beyond the exotic

Pokémon it might contain in its virtual equivalent world. What was its history? What had her own mother done here years before? Who had been coming to visit in more recent years, treading along the same path she and Charlotte were walking now? Sarah wondered if her great-aunt had made it out here often. Now her family was living in her house, sleeping in her beds, and exploring on her island. It gave Sarah a strange feeling.

Sarah's phone vibrated. Charlotte's followed an instant later. Both girls looked down and saw a distinctive orange shape had materialized in the forest just in front of their position. It had a large head, big black eyes, and a red tail that was lit like a match.

"*There's* our Charmander," Charlotte said triumphantly. "I *knew* we'd find it."

Then Sarah, in tones somewhat less exuberant, said: "What's that?"

"I just said it's a Charmander," Charlotte told her. "All that's left to do is catch it."

"No," Sarah said, placing a hand on her friend's shoulder. "I mean . . . what's *that?*"

Charlotte looked up from her screen and saw Sarah pointing down the dirt path. Ahead of them, the trail seemed to widen into a clearing. Inside the clearing, just visible in the gloom cast by the gnarly trees, was . . . something like a pile of stones. Maybe it was a pit for barbecuing? Maybe something else? It was very difficult to see any detail. Whatever it was, it was clearly man-made.

"I guess the island's not totally empty . . . I mean, apart from Pokémon," Sarah said with a grin.

For the first time she could remember, Charlotte looked afraid.

"Do we have to go closer?" Charlotte asked. "I mean, we can catch the Charmander from right here."

"Yeah, but don't you want to see what that is?" Sarah asked. "Maybe it's a place you can have a bonfire. We could come back with hot dogs and marshmallows and have a cookout someday. It would be totally fun!"

"Maybe," Charlotte said hesitantly.

"C'mon," Sarah urged. "We came all this way. Aren't you a little curious?" In her heart, she realized she was saying this as much to herself as to Charlotte. If it was just a cool fire pit on the island and they had been too scared to go near it, Sarah would never hear the end of it . . . *especially* from Skip. And Skip might tell his new friends at school, who would tell other people, and it would just snowball from there.

They couldn't let that happen.

"I . . . I suppose I could go a little closer, just to see what it is," Charlotte said. "It's just . . . something about it makes me uneasy. Why would you put a bunch of stones in the darkest part of an island, where the trees were the thickest? If you were going to build a place for bonfires, why wouldn't you build it out on the beach?"

"Let's go find out," Sarah said, and headed down the path. Charlotte reluctantly followed.

It was so dark underneath the tree canopy that Sarah had to turn on her phone and use the glowing face like a flashlight. She trained her light on the rocks. There were lots and lots of them. Someone had arranged them in a large circle, almost as large as the clearing itself. There were rocks *within* the circle, too. Some had been piled into the shape of a large letter *C* that faced another letter *C*. Then inside of the *C*s more rocks had been added to form a perfect orb.

"Wow," Sarah said. "This must have taken someone a lot of work. They must have used half the rocks on the island to make this design! I wonder if it has a purpose. It can't be for making campfires, because the middle is full of stones too!"

Suddenly, Sarah began to have the uncanny feeling that she had seen this arrangement of rocks somewhere before. Something about it was *familiar*. The answer was on the tip of her tongue. Then, Charlotte spoke.

"It's a PokéStop," Charlotte said quietly.

"Oh yeah!" Sarah said, the pieces suddenly falling into place in her mind. "The rocks are arranged in the shape of an unfurled PokéStop. That's so cool!" Then Sarah's enthusiasm began to flag. "But wait . . . Why would anyone do that? Even if you were a big fan of the game, think of all effort it would take. And to do it here, in the darkest part of an island where nobody would ever see."

"Sarah . . ." Charlotte said, her voice beginning to tremble.

"Does this place still make you nervous?" Sarah asked. "Okay, we can leave. It makes me feel a little weird, too. Not exactly nervous, but like I have a lot of questions now."

"*Sarah*. . ." Charlotte's said again.

"I heard you," Sarah said. "Fine. We're leaving now."

"Sarah . . . what's that thing in the center of the rocks?" Charlotte managed to say, her voice now little more than a whisper.

To Sarah's surprise, Charlotte began to approach the stones. She crossed the outer ring of the enormous PokéStop and moved toward its center. Sarah followed, a bit confused.

"What? What do you see? I don't see anything. I—"

But then she did.

The PokéStop wasn't composed of rocks. Not entirely. At the very center of the formation was a sphere a little larger than a softball. Half of it had been painted white, and the other half red. There was a block stripe running down the center of it, separating the two colors. In the center of the stripe appeared to be a button. Its surface might have been plastic or metal, or might have been something else entirely. It looked hard and shiny, like a beetle's shell.

For a long time, neither of the girls said anything.

"It looks like . . ." Sarah eventually managed.

"I *know* what it looks like," Charlotte said.

Sarah was still trying to wrap her brain around what they were seeing. "But why would . . ." she stammered. "I mean, it couldn't *really* be . . . You don't suppose that . . ."

As Sarah hemmed and hawed, a noise came through the trees from the far side of the clearing. It took both of the girls a long moment to understand that it was coming from an animal.

"Is that a dog?" Charlotte asked. "Is there a dog on this island? A big dog with a growl that's super deep and super loud?"

They heard the sound again. It seemed to shake the leaves on the trees around them.

"Sarah, I don't think we should be here," Charlotte whispered. "I don't know what it is, and I don't know why it has this stuff from Pokémon GO, but I don't think it's for us. We need to go back to the boat and head to land, and I think we should do that *right now*."

Charlotte didn't wait for Sarah to agree. She began backing out of the clearing, away from the direction from which the growl had come. When she reached the clearing's edge, she turned and sprinted down the dirt path.

Sarah took a deep breath. The growl of whatever lurked in the trees was indeed terrifying. It seemed to make her feet shake inside her shoes—to radiate up from the ground, itself. But Sarah thought again about how she didn't want to have come all this way for nothing, and how she might never have an opportunity like this again.

Summoning all her courage, she charged the rest of the way *forward* to the center of the clearing. She stopped abruptly—her feet skittering on the rocks below—and stooped down to grab the red and white sphere. It was hard, but not heavy. Its surface—aside from the button—was perfectly smooth. Sarah hastily stuck the item down the front of her life vest.

"RWAAAAAR," came the growl from the nearby trees. Even the rocks at her feet seemed to shake.

Sarah turned and followed Charlotte. She stumbled across the rocky face of the PokéStop, then broke into a proper run as soon as her feet hit the dirt trail. The growling continued from behind her. She could not seem to get away from the sound. It was almost as if the source of the growl was now *following* her.

And, something else. Something in the air. At first, Sarah thought it might just be the smell of her own fear. But no. There was a distinct *burning* smell in the woods around her. Even though nothing she could see appeared to be on fire, there was the distinct odor of something consumed by flame.

Up ahead, Sarah could see the trees give way to the sunny beach beyond. She had no guarantee that she'd be any safer from whatever pursued her once she reached the sunlight, but something told her it would still be an improvement over staying in the dark woods. She sprinted as though her life depended on it.

Out on the beach, Charlotte was already inside the boat. She held both paddles and was looking back toward the woods, waiting for Sarah.

Sarah sprinted out onto the beach. Immediately, the fire-smell was replaced by the smell of the sea. The strange, suffocating quiet that had muffled all other noise—and allowed her to hear the growling all the more clearly—receded in the rumble and spray of the surf.

"Let's go," Charlotte shouted. "We're getting out of here."

"Coming!" Sarah shouted back, as she raced across the rocky beach.

Sarah reached the little boat and hopped inside. Charlotte thrust a paddle at her. They pushed off into the water and began to paddle furiously for the mainland. They didn't look back.

The Pokémon watched them go.

"Did you girls have a nice time on the island?" Sarah's mother called out before their boat had even reached the beach.

Charlotte and Sarah looked at each other. They realized they had not rehearsed what they were going to say. And now, there wasn't time.

They paddled the boat forward until it made a familiar scraping sound against the rocks. Sarah's mother stood up from her lawn chair and helped pull the vessel to shore. Sarah and Charlotte carefully climbed out. Both girls were still breathing hard with fear and excitement. Fortunately, Sarah's mother mistook this for the effects of good old-fashioned exercise.

"It's a nice row isn't it?" Sarah's mother said cheerfully. "And farther than it looks! I remember my days of rowing out and then back in. I'd have strong arms by the end of the summers here."

Sarah and Charlotte laughed nervously and helped pull the boat the rest of the way out of the water.

"Well, you two are certainly tight-lipped," Sarah's mom continued. "Did you have a nice time exploring, or what?"

"It was . . . okay," Sarah said, failing to return her mother's stare.

"Yeah, it was definitely okay," Charlotte echoed.

"What did you see?" Sarah's mother asked. "Did you discover anything interesting?"

"Not much," Sarah said. "There were some old rocks and stuff. Not much else. It was pretty much what we expected to find."

Sarah worried that her mother would press for even more details. Sarah hated lying, or even telling half-truths. She knew it was a bad thing to do. At the same time, something told her that the encounter she and Charlotte had just had was the sort of thing you *really* didn't want to go blabbing about to adults.

To Sarah's great relief, her mother seemed willing to save her questions for another day.

"Well, if you girls are finished in the water for the day, I'm going to stop being a lifeguard and go back to being a quilter. My shop opens soon, and I still have to race just to have enough quilts to open with. You girls have fun and stay safe."

Sarah assured her mother they would.

"I guess we should take the boat back before my parents get home," Charlotte said.

She and Sarah began to carry it up the path away from the beach. With Sarah's mom far ahead of them on the path, it was their first opportunity to speak about what they had experienced.

"I'd always heard bad things about that island," Charlotte said. "You know. Scary rumors. People calling it Ghost Island, and stuff. But I never thought the rumors could be true."

"What do you think those rocks were?" Sarah asked. "And why did somebody put them into the shape of a PokéStop? It's almost like they knew we were coming."

Charlotte replied, "I'm more interested in what was making that horrible growling sound. When

I was running back to the boat, I felt like it was chasing me. Like, on purpose."

"Yeah," Sarah agreed. "I felt that way, too."

"And also," Charlotte said. "That red and white thing! It looked just like . . . Just like . . ."

Sarah stopped walking and set down her half of the boat. Charlotte seemed confused, but did the same thing. Sarah glanced cautiously up the trail. Her mother had reached the house and disappeared inside. Sarah looked back down at the empty beach, and then at the surrounding hills. There didn't appear to be a soul in sight.

Confident they were alone, Sarah reached down into her life vest. "I think you mean this," she said, handing the red and white orb to Charlotte.

"You *took* it!" Charlotte said in astonishment.

Sarah nodded.

"What if it belongs to that growly thing that chased us? What if it *wants it back*?"

Sarah just shrugged. Taking the ball had been an impulsive act. Charlotte quickly pushed it back at her. Sarah accepted and hid it once more in her vest. They picked up the boat and continued walking.

"Do you think it's a real Poké Ball?" said Charlotte. "It *couldn't* be . . . could it?"

"That's a good question. I think if we throw it at a Pokémon and the Pokémon gets sucked inside, then it's a real Poké Ball."

"But I don't know where any Pokémon are."

"We could always throw it at your babysitter Karen," Sarah suggested. "If she's in the middle of texting her boyfriend, she might not even notice."

Charlotte laughed. "Or we could throw it at Shelley, my dog. She's a mutt, made up of all different kinds of breeds. She's kind of like a Pokémon herself."

To Charlotte's surprise, Sarah said, "You know, that's actually not a bad idea."

"Are you serious?" asked Charlotte. "But what if it . . . um, you know . . . *works*? What if Shelley gets sucked inside? I don't know if dogs like being inside of Poké Balls?"

"Then we'll just use the ball like we're having a Pokémon battle and let Shelley out again," Sarah said. "I bet it will be a fun adventure for her."

Charlotte didn't seem quite so sure.

When they reached Charlotte's house, neither of her parents had returned home yet. The girls stowed the boat back in the shed and took off their life vests. Charlotte's family kept a stack of old shopping bags in the corner of the shed. Charlotte gave one of the bags to Sarah to carry the Poké

Ball. Then they went inside and found Karen on the couch watching television.

"How was boating, or whatever?" she asked without looking up. "More importantly, how is the boat? You *better* not have damaged it."

"The boat is fine," Charlotte replied. "Don't you have more important things to do than quiz us? Shouldn't you be texting?"

"My phone is charging," Karen said. "The stupid battery never lasts long enough. They need to make phones better."

"Hey, where is Shelley?" Charlotte asked.

"I don't know where your dumb dog is," Karen answered. "Probably in the backyard where you left her."

"Okay," said Charlotte. "We'll be outside playing with her for a while."

"What*ever*," said Karen, still staring at the TV.

Charlotte and Sarah moved through the house and the sliding glass doors that opened on the backyard. There they found Shelley lazing in the shade where the roof was casting a shadow. Shelley was an old dog. Her active years were far behind her. The dog looked at the two girls, but did not lift her head.

"Okay," Charlotte said excitedly. "Try to catch Shelley with the Poké Ball."

Sarah took the Poké Ball out of the shopping bag, stood about five feet from the mutt, and prepared to throw. Then she hesitated.

"What?" said Charlotte. "What's wrong? Throw the ball."

"It just doesn't feel . . . like much of a challenge, you know?" Sarah replied. "Shelley's just lying there."

"Plenty of Pokémon just lie there," said Charlotte. "Weedle and Caterpie keep their bellies against the ground, just like Shelley is. And Bellsprout are practically attached to the ground. They literally have roots."

"I know," said Sarah. "But at least they kind of wiggle back and forth a little. Shelley's just lying there. She's not even wagging her tail. And what if it hurts her?"

"C'mon," urged Charlotte. "What if you throw it very gently?"

Sarah sighed.

"Okay," she said. "But I'm gonna throw it *gently*, like you said."

Sarah took a deep breath and whispered, "Sorry, Shelley." Then she reared back like a pitcher and let the Poké Ball fly. It careened through the air and landed against Shelley's thick fur with a muffled thud, then rolled into the grass and stopped.

Shelley looked over at Sarah for a moment—with an expression which seemed to say, *What was* that *about?*—then returned her gaze to the lawn in front of her. Nothing else happened. The Poké Ball did not capture the dog. It did not beep or vibrate. It did not do anything at all.

"Oh," Charlotte said. "I guess it doesn't work after all."

"I think it didn't work because Shelley is a dog, not a Pokémon," said Sarah.

"You're right," admitted Charlotte. "Sometimes, when she comes back from the groomer and her fur is all puffed up, she looks kind of like an Arcanine, but I don't think that counts."

Sarah suddenly became aware that the Poké Ball was now exposed in the grass. Not wanting Karen, or any other wandering eyes to see it, she swiftly put it back in the grocery bag.

"So what are you going to do with it?" Charlotte asked.

"I dunno," said Sarah, closing the bag tight around the ball. "I guess I'll hang on to it. I should probably be getting home now."

"Yeah, okay," Charlotte said. "I don't know about you, but I think I need some time to relax after what we saw today. I'm going to take a long bubble bath and probably go to bed early."

Sarah, who made it a point to negotiate for later and later bedtimes whenever possible, could hardly believe that she agreed with Charlotte, but she absolutely did. With the Poké Ball safely hidden, Sarah left Charlotte's house and headed straight home, not even bothering to play Pokémon GO along the way. Between discovering a PokéStop made of rocks, running from a growling monster, and finding what just might be an honest-to-goodness Poké Ball, Sarah had had a long day.

When she reached her house, she went to her bedroom, hid the Poké Ball at the bottom of her sock drawer, and climbed into her bed. The sun had not yet set, but the moment she closed her eyes, Sarah fell instantly into a deep, dreamless sleep.

PART THREE

several days passed. Sarah's mother worked frantically to stitch enough quilts to open her store. Sarah had not seen her mother this anxious and distracted in a long time. Sarah was kind of anxious and distracted, herself. What had happened on the island seemed like a dream. Like something she had imagined that couldn't possibly have happened for real. But whenever this feeling began to overtake her, Sarah just reached inside her sock drawer and verified its contents. There, beneath the layers of ankle socks and soccer socks, was an actual Poké Ball. There could be no doubt about it.

What unnerved Sarah was that this strange, astounding place—with its growling monsters and real Poké Balls—was not in some far-off place she had visited by car or airplane. It was right behind her house. She saw it every day whenever she looked out of an east-facing window. It was *so close*.

The final, and perhaps most jarring, impact of her adventure to the island was that it completely removed Sarah's desired to play Pokémon GO— at the least for the moment. Skip pronounced this "crazy" and reminded Sarah that he would "totally take every gym in the neighborhood" if she ceased to play. Remarkably, Sarah has seemed fine with this. Skip began to wonder if something might be seriously wrong with his sister.

Then, one night, it happened . . .

Sarah returned home from school on an afternoon that was dull and overcast. The weather had started to turn cool. There was a hint of autumn in the air. The winters back in Chicago had been cold, but everyone told Sarah that in Northern Maine, it would be positively arctic. She knew she would be breaking out a winter coat sooner rather than later.

After dinner, she helped her increasingly-nervous mother stack some fresh quilts and load them into boxes. The store was opening soon. When they finished, Sarah did her homework and watched TV. For a moment, she considered playing a bit of Pokémon GO before the sun set—which was now happening earlier and earlier—but she was still haunted by the same uncomfortable feelings she'd had since her visit to the island. She went up to her room and got into bed, read a book, and fell asleep.

She didn't remember her dreams precisely— though they certainly must have been intense, because she woke from them with a start. She looked over at the glowing face of her alarm clock and saw that it was one minute after midnight.

Something was wrong. She knew that immediately.

From her position in her bed, it was difficult to look around and confirm this, but it seemed certain that something was different in her room. Disturbed. Off.

It took a moment for Sarah to realize what it was.

On the floor, halfway between the bed and the door, was a single white gym sock. One of hers. She always put all of her dirty clothes in a hamper down in the laundry room, and she wasn't the kind of person to kick a sock onto the floor and forget about it.

Sarah switched on the lamp on her nightstand and slowly got out of bed. In the glow, the sock looked clean and without so much as a wrinkle. Unworn. Then Sarah's eyes went from the sock to the sock drawer, which was ever-so-slightly ajar. And Sarah *always* made a point to close it.

Sarah practically leapt to the sock drawer and threw it open. She thrust her hand inside and felt . . . only *socks*.

It was gone.

More precisely, someone had *taken* it. Sarah was certain. But who? She immediately suspected Skip because, well, he was generally behind most things that annoyed her.

Yet this was different, Sarah quickly realized. Skip didn't even know that the Poké Ball existed. No one did, except for Charlotte. And why would *she* take it? Would Charlotte sneak into another family's house in the middle of the night and steal something from another person's room? She didn't seem like that kind of person. And Sarah had never told Charlotte that she was keeping the Poké Ball in her sock drawer. She hadn't told anybody that.

Alarmed and bewildered—and also still quite sleepy—Sarah walked over to the sock in the middle of the floor and picked it up. Intending to return it to the drawer, she happened to glance through her cracked bedroom door out into the hallway. There, she saw something small and white atop the carpet. Sarah walked out to the hallway.

It was, indeed, another one of her socks. One she recognized. It had a tear in the toe and she had been meaning to throw it away for a while. Sarah bent down and picked it up. Then she looked around nervously. The house was dark and quiet; her mother and her brother fast sleep in their rooms. What was going on?

From where she stood in the hallway, Sarah could see down the staircase. And at the bottom was . . .

"Another sock," Sarah said, then suddenly clamped both hands to cover her mouth. She didn't want to wake the rest of her family . . . not until she understood exactly what was going on.

Sarah crept down the staircase, taking each step carefully, trying to be as quiet as possible. She was lucky that the stairs were carpeted.

At the foot of the stairs, Sarah found one of her blue soccer socks, extra large so you could pull it up over your shin guard. She still didn't know what to make of it, but picked it up and added it to her collection. She surveyed the ground floor of the house, squinting to see into the gloom. One of the appliances in the kitchen kicked on and startled her. And that was when she saw it.

Another sock . . .

Outside.

Through the glass panes in the back door, Sarah spied a white sock. It was sitting on a decorative stone that marked the beginning of the path down to the water. *And to the island*, Sarah thought.

She realized that she'd have to make a crucial decision. Would she do the responsible thing— turn on the lights, wake up her mother, and say that there was a sock-stealing so-and-so somewhere in the neighborhood? Or would she do the thing that she desperately wanted to do, even though it scared her? Would she quietly let herself out the back door and follow wherever this trail of socks might lead?

As Sarah looked out the window and tried to make up her mind, a gust of wind tousled the sock, making it look almost alive.

The socks couldn't have crawled down here on their own. The thought screamed inside of Sarah's mind. It insisted on its own truthfulness, but perhaps only because the alternative was too unthinkable. There *had* to be an explanation for this.

Sarah couldn't ignore the mystery. She opened the back door and stepped out into the cool, breezy night.

Sarah quietly closed the door behind her, making sure that it did not lock. She could smell the water and hear the sea lapping against the rocks below. She went over to the decorative sock on the rock and picked it up. She now had so many that she took the largest sock and stuffed the others inside it. She swung it back and forth a couple of times, and thought how satisfying it would be to bop Skip on the head with the bundle. Then she started down the path toward the water, walking slowly. This was not only because the way was steep, but because she knew what she was likely to find. And after a couple of minutes, she did—another sock.

Dropped right in the middle of the path. Sarah picked it up and added it to her sock-bopper. The bopper grew slightly larger.

Along the way down to the water she found four more socks. One of them—part of a Halloween costume featuring shiny silvery embroidery—positively glimmered in the moonlight. Sarah picked them all up. Whether she did it to remove the evidence of whatever was happening, or because she just wanted her socks back, was unclear even to her. She moved mechanically and carefully. She didn't know where the trail was leading, or what she would discover when she got there.

When she arrived at the water's edge, she expected something—or even some*one*—to be waiting there, but she found that she had the rocky beach to herself. Nothing. Silence. She looked across the water at the island, dark and mysterious. She thought about what she had seen and heard there, and shuddered.

Then something caught her attention. Something down the beach. Sarah began walking toward it. Just a few paces from the end of the path was a familiar shape. It was the destroyed, moldy, overturned row boat. The one her mother had used so many years before. And the Poké Ball was sitting on top of it.

Sarah walked up to the boat and carefully took the ball.

"How did you get down here?" she said, almost as if the ball were alive. "Did you roll all this way, or did someone—"

Sarah stopped mid-sentence. Something on the wind made her fall silent. A smell.

It was that same fiery scent that she and Charlotte had smelled on the island that had accompanied the beastly growling. Sarah grew very still and clutched the Poké Ball to her chest. The wind was strong, but with increasing dread Sarah realized that the wind was not blowing in off of the water. Instead, it was blowing down the beach . . . from behind her. The source of this stench was not on the island now, it was on the beach. *With* her.

Very slowly, Sarah turned around.

A Charmander stood there waiting.

The creature stood on its hind legs about five paces from her. It was two feet tall, and had the proportions of a medium-sized dog. Its skin was a strange shade of reddish brown. It looked up at her with enormous blue eyes that twinkled when the moonlight caught them. At the end of its short tail was a single flame about the size of a candle. The tiny blaze fluttered softly in the breeze. The

Charmander opened its mouth—perhaps only to smile—exposing two enormous upper teeth.

Sarah shrieked and instinctively threw whatever was in her hands, which happened to be the Poké Ball.

Powered by Sarah's terror and surprise, the orb sailed through the air in a white-and-red blur. It struck the Charmander directly between the eyes. The Pokémon did not look displeased, but did seem a surprised. An instant later, there was a flash and the Poké Ball opened. The Charmander—which was already not all *that* large—miraculously shrunk so small it could have fit in Sarah palm. At the same time, some unseen force vacuumed it into the waiting Poké Ball. The ball closed over it, and made a satisfying click. Then the ball fell to the ground. It vibrated once, twice, and then a third time. The button on the side of the Poke Ball glowed. Then this glow faded away.

Sarah looked on in amazement. She'd caught a Pokémon. That was the only explanation.

Sarah carefully approached the ball and picked it up from the rocky beach, half-afraid the Charmander might explode back out of it. But nothing happened. The Poké Ball was just as it had been, even with a Charmander inside. The Pokéball wasn't any heavier.

Sarah looked down at the ball in her hands. "What on earth is happening?" she said to herself.

A voice nearby whispered back, "Do you *really* want to know?"

It took Sarah a moment to realize that it was Alice, her elderly neighbor. She was standing on the other side of the overturned boat. Her expression was serious and intense. She didn't look like she was out for a midnight stroll on the beach. She looked like she'd come there with a purpose. She stepped around the boat, and took the Poké Ball from Sarah's hand. Alice held it up and inspected it. She put it beside her ear and shook it, listening intently. Then she smiled and handed to Poké Ball back.

"Nice work," Alice said. "I'm so pleased."

"Pleased?" asked Sarah. "What are you talking about? Also, am I crazy, or did I just see a *real* Pokémon?"

"You did more than just see it," Alice replied brightly. "You caught it. Which is exactly what I was hoping you'd do. We worried that skill Pokémon GO might not translate to the real thing. Evidently, there was no reason for our concern. You caught a Pokémon with your first cast of a Poké Ball. Not a Great Ball. Not an Ultra Ball. Not a Master Ball. A Poké Ball. This bodes well, indeed."

"I don't understand," Sarah said. "I threw that ball because I was scared. I wasn't even trying to hit the Pokémon!"

"You will understand soon," Alice said mysteriously.

"Understand what?" Sarah protested.

"Let's take a little walk together down the shore," Alice suggested. "I'll explain along the way."

"Please do," said Sarah, "because all of this is beginning to make me feel like I'm going crazy."

"You're not," Alice assured her, and began to saunter down the beach. For an older woman, she kept up a very brisk pace. Sarah followed after her.

"The island behind your home is a special place," Alice said, taking a moment to glance out across the water at it.

"I knew *that* already," Sarah insisted. "I went out there and explored. Something chased us, and I saw some stones in the shape of a PokéStop."

"They are not always in the shape of a PokéStop," Alice told her. "Other times, they can be in the shapes of things having to do with other games. Games for kicking or throwing balls. *Or horseshoes.* They have been arrayed like a board for playing chess, or for other, older games, brought here by the first people on this continent."

"This explanation isn't making things any clearer for me."

"Then let me speak as plainly as I can," said Alice. "The island is haunted. Magical. Thin."

Sarah got the first two, but wondered if she'd heard correctly when it came to the third. "Thin?"

Alice nodded seriously, as if this might be its most important attribute of all.

"Reality on the island is thin," the old woman continued. "It is a place where things from other places can come through to our world. Things from other realms. Other realities. And they do . . . every few years. These things that come through—these visitors—they like to play games."

"Games like Pokémon GO?" said Sarah.

Alice nodded, as though to say Sarah was catching on. "This time they want to play Pokémon GO," Alice said.

"Oh, well that should be okay, shouldn't it?" said Sarah. "Everybody can play Pokémon GO, right? The more the merrier."

"I wish I could say that was so," Alice replied seriously, "but these visitors, they like to play for stakes."

"What does that mean?" asked Sarah.

"It means that if they win they get something."

"What do they get?"

"To come into our world," explained Alice. "And that would be a *very* bad thing. Hundreds of years ago, they tried to come through for the first time. The people who lived on that island made a wager with them. A bet. The visitors would have to beat them at a game in order to come through. If the visitors lost the game, then they would go away for thirty years. It is not known what original game the humans played, but they won. And so have humans won each of the ten times since we have played them."

"Who gets to choose the game?" Sarah asked.

"It alternates," said Alice. "The only rule is that is must be a game from our universe. This year, the outsiders have chosen. And the game they have chosen is Pokémon GO."

"No way!" said Sarah, hardly believing her ears. "Why?"

"We don't know everything about where they come from," admitted Alice. "Their plane of existence is different from ours—strange. But I have the sense that they come from a place where Pokémon can exist in such a way that you and I would call them . . . *real*. Perhaps they feel this gives them an advantage."

"And the Pokémon I just caught?" Sarah said.

"An example that slipped through where it's thin," Alice confirmed.

Sarah's head felt like it was spinning. She had already seen—and apparently caught—one real Pokémon, but the idea of a place full of them make her feel weak in the knees.

"But we have advantages, too," Alice continued. "For example, we have millions of humans playing Pokémon in various forms. Pokémon GO is only the most recent. But it is well-timed. The island knew it needed someone special to represent our side. Humanity's side. We should be thankful that it brought you here."

"The island didn't bring me here," Sarah said. "I brought myself to it. I rowed over."

"But what brought you to this place?" asked Alice. "To Clybourne, Maine?"

"My mother did, silly," said Sarah. "She inherited our house. Plus, she thought it would be a good place to open up a quilt shop."

"All these things brought you here, don't you see?" said Alice. "There are no coincidences. Not when it comes to the island. I know this because it was a similar string of *coincidences* that brought me here back in . . . Well, I'm not going to tell you just how old I am, but let's just say it was a long time ago."

"You were one of the people who played against the others?" Sarah asked.

Alice nodded solemnly.

"I have stayed because it is my wish to help people who have been selected after me. People . . . like you."

Sarah cocked her head to the side and made a face like she smelled something strange. "Excuse me, but why would a . . . supernatural force from another dimension choose me to play Pokémon against? That makes *no* sense."

"I have been learning the ins and outs of the game, in preparation for your arrival," Alice began slowly. "So let me ask you some questions to help make it clear. I hope I use all the terms correctly. First of all, what level are you?"

Sarah answered.

"And how many Pokémon have you caught?" Alice asked.

"All of them," Sarah said. "They're always adding new ones to the game, but I get those almost immediately, too. Yes, I'm pretty confident I have all the Pokémon."

"And when you battle at gyms?"

"I always win," Sarah said. "I mean . . . every once in a while, if Skip has stocked a gym, it can give me a bit of trouble, but generally there's nothing that stops me. I'm great at keeping track of which Pokémon are strong against other Pokémon. You might say I've got it down to a science."

"And yet, despite all of these things, it has never occurred to you that you might be the finest Pokémon GO player in the world?"

If Sarah had been drinking something, she would have spat it out. "Me!" she said, not believing her ears. "No way. The designers who built the game are better! There are top-level players with their own YouTube channels. I'm just a kid who plays Pokémon GO a lot."

"And who has captured every Pokémon, and who never loses?"

Sarah stopped for a moment to consider if this could possibly be true. "The thing is, Skip started playing right when I did—the day Pokémon GO came out, more or less," Sarah said. "And if I have trouble beating his gyms . . . If what you're saying is true, Skip would also have to be . . ."

"Also one of the best Pokémon GO players in the world," Alice informed her. "I know you might have mixed feelings about your brother, but I'm afraid it's true."

A moment before, Sarah would have said nothing could be harder to believe than her being the greatest player. But the idea that Skip was up there with her was positively hard to swallow.

Alice looked up at the sky and sniffed the night air. Or had it become early morning air? They had walked and talked for a long time.

"I will need to leave you soon, and you ought to be getting home," said Alice, "so listen. There is still more to tell, and I haven't long. Your skilled brother is also, I think, not a coincidence. And this is why. For the first time ever, the others have asked that instead of one player from our side, there be *three*. They will send three players also."

"Does it have to do with the three Pokémon GO teams?" Sarah asked.

"Very perceptive," said Alice. "That's correct. We have Team Mystic, Team Valor, and Team Instinct. In their world, they have their own teams with their own colors. Because of this, we will need our three representatives to come one from each team. You have been selected as the captain of your team. You must choose those who will stand with you against the others."

Suddenly, it was all clear to Sarah.

"I'm Team Mystic," Sarah said. "My brother's Team Instinct. And my new friend, Charlotte . . . I don't know what level she's at . . . but she's Team Valor. Charlotte is also very, very good."

"Sounds like you've got it all figured out," Alice said with a grin.

"So what happens next?"

The smile fell from Alice's face. "You will be contacted. Summoned at the correct time. They should also summon the others you name to play with you. I'm a little less clear on that part. This is the first time we've had multiple players. But be ready. It will happen soon. The contest is always in the fall. And sense how the air smells tonight, will you? Autumn is on the wind. The great contest is almost ready to come once again."

Sarah had one final question bobbing about in the back of her brain. One final question that she felt like she really, *really* shouldn't ask out loud.

But she did, anyway.

"What if I . . . don't want to?"

"Pardon me?" said Alice.

"This game of playing Pokémon GO against strange creatures from another world . . . What if I don't want to do it? Because maybe I don't."

"My child, do you think that any of us drawn here over the ages have *wanted* to do this?" Alice said. "Nobody *wants* this. But when you have the feeling that the universe has selected you—out of everybody else on the planet—to compete on behalf of your world, you tend to do it."

"Hmm," Sarah said. "I guess so."

Secretly though, Sarah was not sure at all that any of this was something that she wanted to do. It sounded exciting, yes, but also frightening. And if Alice was telling her the whole truth, then there was quite a bit at stake.

Before she could think about it any further, Alice turned to leave. "I need to go," she said. "You should get home, too. Let yourself in the house quietly so you don't wake your mother. She doesn't need to worry about this. No one needs to know except for you. As soon as possible, you should inform those whom you have selected to be on your team."

Sarah nodded.

"Then hurry along, dear," Alice said. "Get some sleep. In the days ahead, you're going to need it."

The next morning, no one noticed that Sarah had been out of the house for a good part of the night, or that many of her socks were crumpled into one big ball at the foot of her bed. Nor did they notice that something heavy weighed on her mind. Something *very* heavy.

How do you ask your bratty brother and your new friend to join you in a supernatural Pokémon

GO contest against aliens from another dimension? And also, how do you do this, and not have them think you're completely nuts?

While she walked to school alongside Skip, Sarah thought about bringing it up then and there—but the moment never seemed right. Also, was it something you told someone right before homeroom? Skip would probably need a while to process this. (It had taken Sarah most of the night, and she still felt pretty freaked out.)

In the end, Sarah hatched a plan. She wrote a note and slipped it into Skip's backpack when he wasn't looking. The note said that someone had something very important to tell him—this was true, Sarah reminded herself—and that he should meet them by the tetherball court directly after school. Later at lunch, when Sarah saw Charlotte, she told her friend that Skip had something important to tell her, and wanted to meet up after school by the tetherball pole. Charlotte thought that was weird, but she didn't say she wouldn't go. Sarah decided this was maybe the best result she could hope for.

When the final school bell rang, Sarah positioned herself in a hidden position near the tetherball court. From where she stood, it would be difficult for anybody heading to the court to see her. Skip was the first to arrive. He made a show of pacing around the tetherball pole, looking for whoever might have left him the note. When nobody immediately showed up, he took out his phone and began to play Pokémon GO.

A few moments later, Charlotte showed up. "What?" she said to Skip.

"Huh?" he replied, putting away his phone.

"What did you want to see me about?"

"I didn't want to see you," Skip said. "Not everything is about *you*, you know. I'm here because . . ."

Sarah stepped out from her cover.

"You're both here because I asked you here," Sarah said. "Skip, I wrote that note. Charlotte, well, sorry for fibbing to you."

Skip and Charlotte exchanged a surprised glance, then they both looked at Sarah for an explanation.

"What is this about?" asked Charlotte. "Does your brother have a crush on me, because *ick*! I am so not going there."

Skip opened his mouth to say something, but Sarah cut him off. "Nobody has a crush on anybody. At least, not that I know of . . . I have something much more important to talk about."

"Why did you need to trick us?" Charlotte asked.

"If I'd told you what this was really about, you would have called me crazy and not shown up."

"As your brother . . ." Skip began mischievously. "I've been around you enough to pretty much say you're crazy for certain. But . . . your friend has a point. What couldn't you tell us?"

Sarah hesitated for a moment. Some things you wanted to tell people gently. Others, you just went ahead and blurted out. Sarah decided that maybe this situation involved the second category.

"There's a magic Pokémon GO contest on the island behind our house, and we've been picked to compete. We have to play against aliens from another dimension. If they win, they get to come through and invade Earth, or something. I'm not one hundred percent clear on that part. Also, that Poké Ball I found on the island—Skip, I didn't tell you that Charlotte and I found a Poké Ball on the island—anyhow, it's real, and last night I used it to catch a Charmander."

Sarah panted, momentarily short of breath.

There was a very. Long. Pause.

Then Skip said: "You went to the island *without me*! You . . . jerks! You *knew* I wanted to go to the island."

"Look, you were playing basketball," Sarah told him. "We couldn't wait for you. We had to use

Charlotte's boat before her parents got home. We would have invited you along, but we were trying to keep on a schedule."

"You're still jerks," Skip decreed, crossing his arms.

Charlotte spoke more carefully. "Wait a minute. When you say you *caught a Charmander*, is that some sort of expression? Like 'I really caught a Charmander on that math test,' or something?"

"No," said Sarah. "More like there was a Charmander down on the beach and I threw the Poké Ball at it, and it sucked the Charmander inside. You know, like how it happens in all Pokémon, ever?"

"Why do *we* have to play against aliens?" Skip asked quickly. "Is it some sort of punishment for something we did?"

"Actually, it's because we're the best players," Sarah said. "You know how you and I have all the Pokémon, and how we're the only ones who can ever steal gyms from each other? That's because there's really nobody out there who can beat us. Except for maybe Charlotte here, which is why she's the third person who'll be coming."

"Coming to what?" Charlotte asked. "When? *I still don't understand anything.*"

"I don't understand all of it, either," Sarah said. "But, apparently, this contest happens soon. Alice—the woman who told me about this—says they're going to come get us and tell us when it's time to go."

"And then we'll have to go play Pokémon GO for real?" said Skip.

Sarah nodded.

"Against aliens, or something?"

She nodded again.

"And if we lose, they do something bad."

Another nod.

"I mean . . . that's fine, I guess," Skip said thoughtfully. "It's just . . . It's just . . ."

"What?" asked Sarah.

"It's just, I still can't believe you went to the island without me! I'll forgive you, but not right away. This is going to take a while. I'm definitely going to be annoyed for a while"

Sarah decided that Skip was taking this about as well as could be expected. Then she looked at Charlotte. She seemed as though she had a million more questions she wanted to ask. But before she could, they were interrupted by the unexpected approach of three people.

"What secret stuff are you guys gossiping about?" a voice asked.

Sarah jumped an inch in her shoes.

"Whoa. I was just joking, but maybe they *are* gossiping about secrets"

Sarah turned to see that it was Richard. He was flanked by Sammy and Maria. Sarah had not seen much of these kids since her first day in town when she'd met Charlotte.

"What do you guys want?" she asked.

"What're you doing back here on the tetherball courts?" Richard asked, if he hadn't heard her question. "Telling more lies about PokéStops on islands that don't even exist?"

"That just shows how much you know," Charlotte fired back. "We found all sort of things on that island. In fact, Sarah was just telling us . . ."

Charlotte noticed Sarah was motioning her to stop talking.

"Oh yeah?" Richard said. "She was just telling you *what*?"

"I was just telling her . . ." Sarah began, trying to think on her feet. "I was just telling her that there might not be any PokéStops on the island, but it's a really fun place to go camping. My mom said so. And we should have a campout there before the weather gets too cold."

Richard stared hard at Sarah for a moment, but said nothing. Then he turned back to his troops. Both of them.

"C'mon Sammy. C'mon Maria. Let's leave these weirdos to be weird together. While they're yapping about nonsense, we can take over another Pokémon gym."

The trio stalked away.

"That was close," Sarah said.

"Yeah," agreed Charlotte. "I haven't been hanging out with them much since school started. In think they're just jealous you're my new friend. Especially, Richard."

"Back to the important stuff," Skip said after Richard and his crew had walked out of earshot. "Supposing that any of the crazy things you have told us are true . . . then what are we supposed to do to get ready?"

Sarah thought for a moment.

"I don't think there's anything we *can* do. They just come for us. And, apparently, they come soon."

PART FOUR

The next night something woke Sarah, but it wasn't aliens from beyond. She opened her eyes and looked at the red face of her alarm clock. Not quite midnight this time. Instinctively, she glanced over to her sock drawer. It did not appear to be disarranged. The Poké Ball was still safe within.

What had awakened her?

For a moment, Sarah wondered if it had just been a dream. Sometimes nightmares could startle her awake, her heart pounding, even if she couldn't recall what she'd been so afraid of. But just as Sarah began to wonder if it might have been one of those, she heard a sound. It was soft and distant, but it was very real. Coming from the other side of the house, a woman was crying. After a few moments of listening, she realized that it was her mother.

Sarah rose from her bed and silently opened the door to her room. The sound was clearer now. There could be no doubt about it. Her mother was down in the kitchen and she was crying.

Sarah crept to the top of the staircase. "Momma," she called down. "Are you okay? Are you hurt?"

Suddenly, a dark possibility occurred to Sarah. What if aliens from another dimension had shown up to ask her to play Pokémon, but they'd startled her mother instead?

Sarah hurried the rest of the way down the stairs.

By the time she entered the kitchen, her mother seemed to have pulled herself together. She was wiping her eyes with a cloth napkin. "Sarah, I thought you were fast asleep. You should be. Tonight's a school night."

"I *was* sleeping . . . but I heard you crying and I got scared. Are you okay?"

"I'm fine," her mother said in a way that made Sarah certain she was not fine at all.

"Why were you crying?" Sarah asked. "Is it something I did? Or Skip?"

Her mother made a brave face. "No, both of you have been angels. You didn't complain when we moved out here, and you've been so good about adjusting and making new friends. You've done more than I ever could have asked."

"What it is then?" asked Sarah.

"Sometimes, adults have problems that make them a little anxious," her mother said. "I want what's best for you and your brother . . . for all of us. I'm just a bit nervous because since it opened, the quilt store hasn't been doing as well as I'd hoped. When the leasing agent showed me the space, she didn't tell me there were already two other quilt stores in the same neighborhood, with very loyal customers. I just want things to go well so I can give you and Skip everything you deserve. But things will turn around soon, I feel sure of it. Please don't worry. I shouldn't have even told you. Now head on back to bed, okay kiddo? I just need to think for a while."

"Okay," said Sarah, and slowly walked back upstairs.

She put herself to bed but couldn't sleep. For some time she continued to listen to her mother softly weeping. The sound stopped after about an hour. Sarah heard the kitchen faucet turning on, and then the refrigerator opening and closing.

Sarah didn't like knowing that her mother was upset. She also disliked that there wasn't anything she could do about it. Sarah racked her brain for a way to help, but nothing came to mind.

Then, just as it seemed to Sarah that she might fall back to sleep, she heard a noise in the hallway. Footsteps. Headed for her room.

The door to Sarah's room slowly *creeeeeeaked* open. Sarah inhaled sharply and looked up.

There was a figure in the dark hallway beyond, but it wasn't her mother. The silhouette was a short, slim figure wearing a baseball cap with no logo and a backpack. A thin boy in his late teens, perhaps. He wore the uniform and demeanor of a Pokémon trainer.

But, at the same time, the figure was none of these things at all. As Sarah got out of bed and moved closer, strange aspects became clear. This person—if indeed it was a person—was not in color. He was rendered in stark black and white, like in an old movie. Even stranger, Sarah realized she could see the wall and the staircase on the other side of the figure, even though he was blocking the door.

As Sarah looked on, the figure beckoned her with its finger, then turned away and descended the staircase in completely silence, as though its feet did not actually touch the carpet below.

Sarah thought she knew what was happening. Tonight was the night!

She quickly got dressed, grabbed the Poké Ball from her drawer, and followed after the strange figure.

On the landing outside of her room, she walked into Skip. "Just so you know," he whispered, "it woke *me* up first."

"I don't think that matters."

"Like how the fact I'm a few seconds older than you 'doesn't matter'?" Skip mused. "Go on, convince yourself that's true."

"Whatever," said Sarah. She followed the figure down the staircase. Skip did, too.

"I've got to say, I thought you might have been lying out on the tetherball court," he said. "But I don't think that now. This is some kind of ghost, or something."

"Yeah," Sarah said cautiously. "Or something."

They followed after the silent figure on a path that was now familiar—out of the house, down the treacherous trail, and to the water below.

"It didn't say anything?" Skip said, nodding at the apparition. "Why doesn't it say anything? If we're going to be playing Pokémon GO, I at least have to know what rules we're gonna use."

"I have a feeling we're going to learn everything we need to know when we get there," Sarah said confidently.

"But where is 'there'?" Skip asked.

Sarah just nodded ahead to the island, now framed in the moonlight.

"Oh," said Skip. "Duh."

The figure led them down the path toward the rocky beach, where they could see Charlotte and Alice standing there waiting for them. In the water sat an old wooden boat—a thin canoe that could hold only three or four people. Charlotte had an anxious, excited, but overwhelmingly pleased look on her face. Alice, on the other hand, seemed impatient. She frowned sternly and wrinkled her already-quite-wrinkly brow.

"Who's the old lady?" Skip whispered as they approached.

"Shh," Sarah snapped. "Don't be rude. That's Alice, the woman I told you about. She lives in the next house down the coast from ours. She's the one who explained to me what was happening with all of this. Well . . . *sort of* explained."

When Sarah and Skip reached the beach, the spectral figure took one step into the water and suddenly vanished in a puff of smoke or water vapor or possibly something else entirely.

"Wow!" said Skip. "That's so cool."

Sarah smiled, then turned her attention to Charlotte and Alice.

"Omigosh, you weren't lying about any of this!" Charlotte said to Sarah. "One of those see-through Pokémon trainers came and got me from my house, too. Except mine was a girl."

Before Sarah could reply, Alice stepped forward, still looking gravely concerned. "Sarah," she began. "And you must be Skip. I've just met Charlotte. Children, we have a problem. Do you know some youngsters about your ages who go by . . . what were the names again . . . Richard, Sammy, and Maria?"

Sarah, Charlotte, and Skip looked at one another.

"Of course we do," Sarah said. "They're kids in the neighborhood. They go to our school."

"They were with me when I first met Sarah and Skip," Charlotte said helpfully.

Alice nodded, but her expression stayed grim. "And tell me, do they also play Pokémon GO?" Alice asked.

"Ha," said Skip. "I think *play* is giving them too much credit. They try to play, but they're light years behind where we are."

"And you told them about the island," Alice said. It was a statement, not a question.

"Only sort of," said Sarah. "They kind of over-heard us talking."

"And I told them how I always used to get a PokéStop to appear on my radar out on the island . . . but it never appeared when they were around," Charlotte added. "Now I think I know why that was."

"Why are you bringing up Richard, Sammy, and Maria?" Sarah asked Alice. "What's happened with them?"

"Something very unfortunate, I'm afraid," Alice told her. "From what I gather, earlier tonight, those three took their own boat out to the island—with the goal of exploring or catching Pokémon or something. Tonight is the night of the great contest, but they didn't know. When they arrived, our guests from the *other side* thought that they were you. They thought that *they* were the three sent to compete with them at Pokémon GO."

"Ohmygoodness," Charlotte said.

"Uh oh." Sarah looked worried.

"But they're not very good at Pokémon," said Skip.

Alice looked down her nose at Skip.

Sarah realized they could have a big problem. "I'm almost afraid to ask, but what happened?"

"The short version is they lost," replied Alice. "They played, and they lost. Badly."

"So what's going to happen?" Sarah asked.

"Well, I've been able to negotiate something on our behalf . . . I think," said Alice.

"You think?" asked Sarah.

"As you can imagine, our guests would like to believe that they've won the competition. "And I don't blame them. But some kids stumbling into where you play the game is not the same as playing against the competitors who were chosen. I think they have some sense of this. They just don't want to admit it. They want an advantage."

"That Richard," Charlotte said to herself. "He's always mucking things up. Now he's ruined our chance to play real Pokémon GO."

"What are we going to do?" Sarah asked.

"That remains to be seen," said Alice. "But we should go to the island quickly. The longer we wait, the more comfortable the others may become with the notion they've already won. Here, get into this boat."

Alice headed for the long wooden canoe.

"You know, there *are* boats with motors," Skip said. "There have been for a long time."

"You might say that this old boat is lucky," Alice remarked as they climbed aboard. "It has brought good fortune every time it's taken a competitor out to the island. And tonight of all nights, I think we need all the luck we can get."

They paddled the canoe out across the water. Sarah had never been inside a boat that was so old. The wood had worn from brown to black, and it seemed a wonder that it was still seaworthy.

Sarah looked for any sign of movement on the island. It appeared that all was calm. But as the canoe neared the shore, Sarah saw that a dim light radiated from the island's wooded center. Sarah didn't know what the light could be, but nothing much could shock her on a night that was already full of surprises.

The group got out of the canoe and dragged it onto the land. Alice set off down the trail that led into the trees. She seemed to know the island well. Sarah began to wonder if it was this mysterious old woman who had kept the trail so well-worn.

"This place is cool," Skip said as they followed Alice under the dark canopy of trees. "And to think you came here without me!"

"What's that light?" Charlotte asked.

"I bet we find out very soon," whispered Sarah.

A very strange sight awaited the group when they emerged in the clearing at the center of the island. The first thing that caught their attention was a single golden lamp, the lone source of illumination. It burned with an eerie green flame that did not seem natural. The lamp was about two feet tall, appeared to be made of real gold, and someone had placed it at the very center of the rocks that formed the PokéStop. It lit up the entire clearing.

Standing to one side of the lamp were some familiar faces: Richard, Sammy, and Maria huddled together as if they were cold. But that made no sense; the night was pleasant and warm. Sarah glimpsed their faces and realized that they were terrified. They looked like kids who were in very big trouble and knew it. Kids waiting to find out how many weeks they were going to get in detention. Kids who had done something very, *very* bad. But when they saw Sarah and the approaching group, their faces lit up and their expressions melted into relief.

Standing on the other side of the stone PokéStop was a group of figures that Sarah had never seen before.

Except she had.

Pokémon trainers. They seemed like every Pokémon trainer she had ever seen in comics or TV shows or web series. They had spiky hair and backpacks that must have been brimming with all sorts of Poké Balls. They were perfect. *Too perfect*, Sarah thought. Too perfect to be real. They were exactly what you would create if you were an alien trying a little too hard to appear to be a Pokémon trainer.

Alice stalked up to the closest Pokémon trainer like she knew him. "Here," she said. "These are the *real* players from our side. The ones I was telling you about."

The Pokémon trainer looked the new group over. Something was wrong with his eyes, Sarah decided. He had assumed the form of a Pokémon trainer in all other ways, but just couldn't get the eyes right. They looked gray and black, but there was no color. For all their bright clothing and accessories, the Pokémon trainers had dead, gray eyes. All of them.

"I see," said the Pokémon trainer after a long inspection. His tone was neutral, as if he did not wish to disclose how he felt. His voice did not match his body, either. It had the deeper timber of an older man—about forty years too old for the body it inhabited.

"So you understand, they must be allowed to play," Alice concluded.

"Our representatives have already played," said the trainer. "And they won. They are exhausted from playing. They cannot be asked to play again. That would not be fair."

Alice sighed. To Sarah, Alice seemed like a law-yer arguing a court case before a difficult judge.

"But they did not play against our represen-tatives," Alice said. "They played against a group of scared kids who didn't even know what was happening."

Sarah looked over again to where Richard, Sammy, and Maria huddled. They certainly did appear to have gone through something very bewildering.

"They showed up to the island at the appointed time," said the trainer. "It was reasonable for us to conclude they had been selected. Why did they appear here, on this night? Why did they know about Pokémon GO? It is almost as though your side did not keep the contest a secret."

Alice glanced over at Sarah, Skip, and Charlotte. All three shrugged.

"Nevertheless," said Alice. "Our team is here now, and they are ready to play."

"And as I have said, *our* team has already played and is tired," said the trainer. "I *wish* we could delay the contest or reschedule it, but you know the rules of the ancient agreement. The contest must take place tonight."

"What if your team had . . . more players?" Alice suggested.

The Pokémon trainer looked intrigued.

"What do you mean?" it said.

"What if instead of playing three-on-three, we were to play you three-on-six?" Alice proposed. "Your team will have twice as many players. That ought to more than make up for some of your players being tired, yes?"

The Pokémon trainer considered this for a moment. He seemed tempted, but wary, as though he was concerned that the proposal might be a trick.

"Your offer is very generous," the trainer eventually said. "And I admit it is appealing. However, an argument could still be made that we have already won the contest. Why should we agree play again if we've already won?"

"Because we will also sweeten the stakes," said Alice.

The Pokémon trainer did not respond beyond blinking a single time. Alice looked hard into his face, almost as though they were having a staring contest. (Sarah and Skip had gone through a phase of having these all the time. Sarah usually won. Usually.)

"Yes," said the trainer. "What is your offer?"

"We will play for the normal stakes," said Alice, "but also for something else."

Alice looked back at Sarah, Skip, and Charlotte for a moment. It seemed to give her confidence. She approached the Pokémon trainer until she stood directly beside him.

"In addition to the regular stakes, if you win the contest . . ." She whispered the rest into his ear.

This time, the Pokémon trainer could not conceal his excitement. His eyebrows lifted in surprise. He stepped back to look Alice in the face.

When she nodded her confirmation, the trainer said, "Very well. And what if your side wins? What then?"

Again, Alice whispered into the Pokémon trainer's ear. He smiled as if her request were a trifle.

"That will be no problem," the trainer said in his eerily deep voice. "Very well. We are agreed."

"Good," said Alice. "I'm glad our terms are acceptable."

"Is your side ready to begin?" asked the trainer.

"Of course," said Alice. "And yours?"

The Pokémon trainer chucked and glanced confidently over his shoulder at the group of trainers standing behind him.

"We certainly are," he said.

"Then just let me give our players their final instructions, and we'll begin," Alice said.

She motioned for Sarah, Skip, and Charlotte to follow her, and walked to the edge of the clearing, where she sat down on a tree stump. The three players-to-be huddled around her like she was a coach outlining a play.

Which maybe she was.

"Okay now," Alice whispered. "Here's where it really begins. I've taken you as far as I can, but from here on out it will be up to you."

"What exactly is going to happen?" Sarah asked.

"You're going to play Pokémon GO against the others," Alice said. "You're going to play it on this island. It has ten gyms on it. You can't see them now, but in a moment you will see *everything*. The first team that controls all ten gyms will win. You play as long as it takes to make that happen."

"But that could mean playing for days," sputtered Skip. "Gyms can change hands quite easily. What if our families miss us? What if we get marked absent from school?"

"Time has a way of passing strangely during a contest," Alice said cryptically. "The others have a version of this island in their home, too. When you play, you will be half in their world, and half in our own. You may find that days have passed for you during the contest, but only minutes have passed on the island."

"Wow," said Skip. "That's insane."

"Oh, it's something all right," Alice mused.

"So if we control all ten gyms, the contest just suddenly ends?" asked Sarah.

"That's correct," said Alice. "You won't battle their trainers directly; you'll use the gyms. It will be just like in Pokémon GO. And you heard what I said to them. Your friends have really mucked things up by coming to this island tonight. Because of their actions, you will be playing against six other trainers, not three."

"That doesn't seem very fair," Skip said. "Why are we getting punished for something Richard and those guys did?"

"Fairness doesn't factor into it," said Alice. "Believe me, the result could have been *much* worse."

Across the clearing, the head Pokémon trainer cleared his throat. "We are waiting," he called to Alice.

Alice nodded hesitantly. "I have to go now, children," she said. "During the game, I will be sort of with you, but sort of not. I don't have time to explain. Just remember that the world brought the three of you together at this moment because you're the very best Pokémon GO players. You were made to do this. Now, go catch some Pokémon. And try and have some fun!"

Alice winked at them. Then she returned to the center of the PokéStop where the strange green flame burned brightest. The children followed.

"Okay, we're ready to begin," Alice said to the Pokémon trainer. "Sarah, Skip, Charlotte—I want you to close your eyes now. We are going to count backward from three. Do not open your eyes again until after we've counted down all the way. Do you understand?"

"Yes," they said in unison.

"Very well," replied Alice. "Then we will begin."

Sarah closed her eyes. Skip and Charlotte did, too.

The clearing grew supernaturally silent, as though all the air had been sucked out of it. Then came the sound of Alice's voice—clear as a bell—as well as the voice of the Pokémon trainer (who was not really a Pokémon trainer, at all). They spoke slowly and in perfect unison.

"Three . . . two . . . ONE."

Sarah opened her eyes.

PART FIVE

They were in a world of wonders.

Sarah was still there. Skip and Charlotte was still there. Most certainly, the opposing team of Pokémon trainers were still there. (Six in total.) But everything else on the island seemed different.

They sky above was bright as though it were midday. There was movement all around them. Set back a few feet into the woods, Sarah could see the revolving interlaced circles of a PokéStop. Towering above them in the sky nearby—slowly rotating on an unseen axis—was an empty gray Pokémon gym, beckoning them to claim it. There was also movement in the forest in several places. Sarah instantly understood what that must mean. *Real* Pokémon, waiting to be captured.

Sarah realized she was wearing a backpack she hadn't been wearing an instant before. Skip and Charlotte were wearing them, too. Sarah pulled hers off her shoulders. She set it on the ground, unfastened a latch at the top, and opened it up. Inside it was brimming with treasures. Sarah began to explore.

First and foremost, there were Poké Balls, just like ones she had used to inadvertently capture the Charmander down on the beach.

"There must be fifty in total," she said to herself. "Just like at the start of the game."

Also inside was a clear glass jar with opaque white ends and what appeared to be a set of controls along the base. With mounting excitement, Sarah realized it was an egg incubator. A *real* egg incubator.

At the very bottom of the backpack were two heavy discs that reminded Sarah of green and white hockey pucks. They each had a button on the side with a glowing yellow light, and a hole in the top. These were incense dispensers, ready to provide the smell of . . . whatever it was that attracted Pokémon. (Sarah was realizing she still had a lot to learn about the new world she was in.)

Sarah glanced over and saw Skip and Charlotte investigating their own backpacks. Each backpack represented the player's team color, yet they all seemed to have identical contents. Skip was holding a Poké Ball in one hand and rubbing his chin with the other, apparently deep in thought.

"You could throw it like a baseball," he mused, "but it's a little big for that. Plus, there aren't any seams to grip. On the other hand, it's a little small to shoot like a basketball. Hey Sarah, how did you throw it when you caught that Charmander?"

"Uh . . ." Sarah said, trying to recall. "I threw it like I was really afraid and startled because I'd just seen a Charmander."

"So . . . overhand or underhand?" asked Skip.

Sarah rolled her eyes.

"This is so cool!" said Charlotte. "Fifty of my very own Poké Balls!"

She had turned her backpack upside down and dumped the contents into a big pile.

"Don't get too attached to them," cautioned Sarah. "Remember, we've got to use them to catch Pokémon."

Skip eyed the slowly rotating PokéStop a few feet into the tree line. He began creeping toward it. As he did, it went *bing* and unfolded welcomingly. Charlotte collected the contents of her backpack and joined him. Sarah walked over, too.

"How do you think it works?" Skip asked.

Sarah and Charlotte shrugged.

Skip shouted at the stop in a loud voice: "Give me some Poké Balls!"

Nothing happened. The PokéStop continued to rotate gently.

"Maybe I have to smack it with my hand," Skip said. "And even if that doesn't work, it will still be fun to do." Skip took the side of his hand and slapped it hard against one of the rotating rings. The ring began to spin madly for a moment as if supernaturally powered. Then, just as suddenly it slowed again, leaving behind three Poké Balls and a very large egg with dark green spots all over it. They top-pled to the soft grass in front of the PokéStop and came to a rest. The PokéStop changed color from blue and purple, and seemed to power down. Sarah understood that it would be exhausted for a while. In the meantime, Skip descended on his booty.

"Awesome!" he said, adding the Poké Balls to his backpack and then carefully picking up the egg. "What do you think's inside? Is it a two kilo-meter egg, or a five? Also, what are kilometers? I was never clear on that exactly. They're like miles but . . . not miles?"

Charlotte said: "This island's not that big. You may have to make several circles around it in order to hatch an egg."

"I know," Skip said defensively. "I'm not stupid. I know how they work."

Skip carefully opened his incubator and put the egg inside.

"Please be a Pikachu, little egg," he said to it as he closed the top and put it back in his backpack.

"I doubt you're gonna get a Pikachu right off the bat," Charlotte said skeptically.

"How do you know?" said Skip. "Have *you* been here before?"

Charlotte was about to open her mouth to argue, but no sound came out. She'd seen something that made her fall silent. After a stunned second, she managed to point just over Skip's shoulder to where the bushes were moving.

A Pokémon was there.

It was long brown wormlike creature with many segmentations that gradually got smaller as they descended down from the creature's head. That head was only vaguely wormlike, and decidedly friendly. It had two large black eyes, a big pink nose in the shape of an oval, and a single conical spike coming out of the top of its head (which looked more like a tiny dunce cap than anything else). It was about a foot tall. When it saw the three friends and reared up off the ground, swaying back and forth.

"Omigosh," Charlotte managed to say. "A Weedle! Someone catch it! I'm not ready yet."

"Eh, it's just a Weedle," Skip said. "I'm not excited."

"How are you not excited?" Charlotte said. "It's an actual, real Weedle hanging out right next to us."

"It's not going to have a lot of CP or be very good at holding a gym," said Skip.

Sarah piped up. "It might be a good way to practice with the Poké Balls. You know, like, decide on a throwing style?"

"Oh," said Skip. "I hadn't thought of that. All right. I guess I'll catch a Weedle."

Skip took out a Poké Ball and hurled it overhand at the Weedle. The creature seemed ready to accept its fate—not taking any steps to conceal itself, just bobbing slightly back at forth. Yet no sooner was Skip's Poké Ball in the air than the Weedle bowed forward, allowing the projectile to sail just over it.

"What?" Skip cried. "No fair. That's cheating."

"It's not cheating," said Charlotte. "The Weedle can do what it wants."

Sarah would not have sworn to it—especially because the Weedle had no mouth that she could see—but it seemed that the Weedle smiled just a little bit when Charlotte said this.

"Whatever," said Skip. "I'll get this stupid Weedle yet."

He took out another Poké Ball and threw with all his might. The Weedle ducked again.

"Darn it!" said Skip.

"Maybe try another approach?" Charlotte suggested.

"Yeah, okay," Skip said, taking up another ball.

The Weedle bobbed back and forth, as if to say, *Bring it!*

Skip took the Poké Ball and did a windup like a baseball pitcher. Then he threw the ball from a sideways position near his hip. This caused the ball to sparkle momentarily.

"Ooh," Charlotte said as the Poké Ball careened through the air. "A sidearm throw. You get extra points for that."

The Weedle flinched at the last moment, but the Poké Ball struck it anyway. The ball popped open and the wormlike creature was suddenly and violently sucked in, shrinking supernaturally until it was just tiny enough to fit.

The ball closed with a click and landed on the grass. It jerked back and forth a couple of times, then went still.

"That's what you get for trying to dodge *my* throws!" Skip said triumphantly.

"Skip, don't gloat," Sarah said.

"Wow, our first Pokémon of the contest," said Charlotte. "What are we going to name him?"

"Name him?" said Skip. "*Name* him?"

"What?" said Charlotte defensively. "You can name Pokémon. It's a totally accepted part of the game."

Skip picked up the full Poké Ball and placed it into his backpack. His expression said he thought Charlotte's naming idea was silly.

"One, it's just a Weedle," Skip said. "Two, it's going straight in a gym, so I won't have time to get attached to it. Three—"

"*Wally!*" said Charlotte. "That would be a good name for him. Wally the Weedle."

"I . . . but . . . fine. Fine. His name is Wally the Weedle. Are you happy now?"

Charlotte nodded enthusiastically. "Sarah, what do you think? I think Weedles should have names that start with *W.* That's just the best way to do it, don't you agree? Sarah?"

But Sarah wasn't paying attention. She was looking across at the other side of the clearing. There, the other team was also getting to work. There were two PokéStops on that side, which they'd already harvested from. Now it looked like they were in the process of catching a Caterpie, which looked somewhat similar to a Weedle, but more wiggly and green.

"Ooh," said Charlotte, following Sarah's gaze. "Clarence the Caterpie. No, wait! Candace. I think I like Candace better."

Sarah ignored her friend for the moment. She was captivated by the opposing team. They had backpacks, but in strange colors she didn't recognize from the game. There was an orange backpack, a purple one, and pink, green, black, and white rounding out the rest. The backpacks seemed like something that fit in the world if you didn't think about it much. But when you did, you realized they didn't belong at all. The alien Pokémon trainers moved mechanically and stiffly, and had those alien, gray eyes. Half were male and half were female, but they were all altogether wrong. They each reminded Sarah of some kind of monster pretending to be a human Pokémon trainer. Then Sarah reminded herself that that was *exactly* what they were—aliens from another dimension who were trying to use Pokémon GO to gain access to her world where they would probably want to do awful, nasty things. But it was their decision to use Pokémon GO that both-ered Sarah most. They had made this *personal*. Sarah had enough problems on her plate. She had just moved halfway across the country to a new town, enrolled in a new school, and her mom was very worried about her struggling quilt shop. The last thing she needed to deal with was playing Pokémon for the fate of the world. As the alien Pokémon trainers captured the Caterpie, Sarah's face contorted into a scowl. She resented the fact she even had to be here. But now, more than ever, she was determined to win.

"Charlotte, we'll talk about giving Pokémon names later," Sarah said. "Skip, let's go ahead and claim that gym before the other team can."

She gestured to the gray gym rotating softly in the center of the clearing, a few feet off the ground.

"Okay," said Skip. "How do I do that?"

"I dunno," said Sarah. "But if we want to win this game, we've got to figure it out fast. Keep in mind, half the guys we're up against have already played this through once. And won. They know where the PokéStops are, and probably where the best Pokémon are hiding. We're at a disadvantage. And I don't know about you guys, but I don't play to lose."

This seemed to rally Skip.

"Me either," he said, and charged over to the Pokémon gym.

Skip took the Poké Ball containing the captured Weedle out of his backpack. He took in the rotating gym, trying to figure out what to do. Across the clearing, the alien Pokémon trainers looked at Skip skeptically. A couple of them even smiled in a way that, to Sarah, seemed mean.

She became even more determined that her team had to win.

Skip held out the Poké Ball and approached the rotating center of the gym. He seemed hesitant, and a little afraid. He waved the ball around in front of the gym. He looked like someone feeding an apple to a very large animal. (An animal that might or might not try to bite your finger in addition to the apple.)

Across the clearing, Sarah saw that some members of the opposing team were now actually laughing.

"Skip," she said, "I've got an idea. Try throwing the Poké Ball into the center of the gym. Not hard. Just lob it in there."

Accepting that his prior efforts had not yet worked, Skip shrugged and threw the Poké Ball with a gentle underhand toss. As if by magic, the gym began to move on its own. It spawned a flat disc floor and caught the Poké Ball. Then the ball opened and the Weedle was revealed. (The Weedle looked excited to be in a gym, and twitched back and forth in anticipation.) Then the disc floated high into the sky—twenty feet or so—and began to rotate slowly, making a proud display of the little Weedle. At the same instant, the color of the gym began to morph from dull grey to a brilliant bright yellow—exactly the shade of yellow of the backpack Skip wore. Beneath the Weedle, two other discs spawned and began rotating quietly. These were for additional Pokémon, Sarah realized. But, for now, they only had the one.

Instantly, the cruel smiles fell from the faces of the alien Pokémon trainers across the clearing. Skip had done it.

Sarah watched the rotating Weedle and smiled. The other team might have more players and experience, but their team had the lead. At least for now. As the frowning alien Poké trainers stalked off into the woods, Sarah noted with pleasure that the good guys were already up one-nothing.

"Awesome," Skip said, backing away from the Pokémon gym. "Good thinking, sis."

"Yeah, that's great," added Charlotte. "We only have to do that nine more times and we win!"

"Correction," cautioned Sarah. "We have to control nine more gyms. The other team will be trying to take them away from us the whole time, too. It's going to be harder than simply repeating what Skip just did."

"Oh," said Charlotte.

"But we can still be happy," said Sarah. "We are in the lead. For now."

The group surveyed the clearing and tried to decide what to do next.

"Should we follow the other team and see what they find?" Charlotte asked.

"Actually, I think we should do the opposite of that," Sarah replied. "It looks like when you catch a Pokémon in this game, it's gone. Taken. Someone else already has it."

"So we should explore the sections of the island they haven't gotten to yet," said Charlotte. "That makes sense."

"But what if they went that way because they know that side of the island has the best Pokémon?" asked Skip.

"I think we've got to hope they're wrong," Sarah said. "And who knows? Maybe each time you play Pokémon GO on this island, the location of the Pokémon resets. That could be the case."

"If that's true—if the Pokémon have changed places since those alien guys beat Richard, Sammy, and Maria—then the other team is going to figure it out pretty quickly," Skip pointed out.

"True," said Sarah. "So we need to catch all the Pokémon we can, while we can. Let's not waste any more time. C'mon!"

Sarah headed into the woods. Skip and Charlotte followed.

"Should we use a lure?" Skip suggested. "Maybe if one of us saw a lure activated, all three of us could benefit from the Pokémon it would bring in."

"That's a good idea," said Sarah.

"Omigosh!" cried Charlotte.

A wild Pidgey had appeared in the bushes just behind her.

"You guys, it's *sooo* cute," Charlotte cooed. She quickly removed her backpack and took out a Poké Ball. The Pidgey shuffled back and forth on its feet and pecked absently at the feathers on its side. Charlotte squared off and prepared to throw. She took her time winding up. The Pidgey gave her a look as if to say, *Are we gonna do this, or what?*

Charlotte threw the Poké Ball.

It connected with the Pidgey with a satisfying *pok* sound. The ball cracked open. The Pidgey began to magically shrink and was quickly drawn inside. The Poké Ball closed again. Charlotte carefully picked it up and put it in her backpack.

"My first real Pokémon!" she said with great satisfaction as they continued deeper into the woods. "What should I name it? Oh, I know. Midge! Midgey the Pidgey!"

"There you go getting all attached again," said Skip.

"You're just jealous because I caught my Pokémon on the first throw," said Charlotte.

"Liking to name my Pokémon doesn't mean I'm not a good Pokémon player. Maybe giving them names makes me *better* at playing."

"You know, Skip, Charlotte might have a point," said Sarah. "Maybe naming your Pokémon is what helped Charlotte get so good. She *did* catch that Pidgey on the first toss."

"Whatever," said Skip. "Name your Pokémon if you want to. Heck, dress them up in clothes like dolls if you want to. It's none of my business. I'll just stick to catching the best Pokémon I can. You do your thing, I'll do mine."

As they continued deeper into the woods. Sarah reached into her backpack and took out one of the puck-shaped containers of incense. She pressed the flat button on the side to turn it on. Almost immediately, a steady stream of sparkly pink smoke began to stream from the small tube sticking out of the top. To Sarah, it smelled like cotton candy and sunshine and pony rides. (She could not recall actually having ever ridden a pony, but she seemed sure that if she did ride one it would smell just like this.)

"Gee," Sarah said, "I see why they like this stuff."

"That smells amazing," Charlotte agreed.

"Maybe you guys are part Pokémon," Skip said.

The girls decided not to respond.

They moved deeper into the underbrush and, almost immediately, a Rattata leapt out. It looked very much like a normal rat—Sarah had definitely seen *those* back in Chicago—but it had a long curly tail held erect, and massive oversized front teeth. The expression of its face said that it had just smelled possibly the nicest thing on earth, and it wanted to be as close as possible to it.

"Stand back," Sarah cried, taking a Poké Ball from her backpack. "I haven't caught one yet. This guy is mine."

Sarah drew back the Poké Ball and looked the Rattata in the eye. Even though it had big teeth, it was not particularly fierce looking. Sarah knew that Rattata could jump out of the way at the last minute—even if they had low CP. She took a careful approach. As the Pokémon bobbed back and forth, looking for the source of the delicious smell, she feinted as though she would throw, but held onto the ball. The Rattata leapt up instinctively, jumping over nothing.

"Aha!" said Sarah. "I thought so."

As the Rattata's feet connected with the ground once more, she let the Poké Ball fly. Her aim was true, and it hit the Rattata right on the nose. There was a satisfying sound as the ball opened and the

Pokémon was sucked inside. The Poké Ball closed, fell to the ground, and lay still. Sarah picked it up and put it in her backpack.

"Matt the Rat," tried Charlotte. "No, wait. Too easy. What rhymes with Rattata?"

"I think I'll leave the naming up to you," Sarah said with a grin.

"Hey, look at that!" Skip called, pointing through the foliage ahead of them. Skip was taller than the girls, so he had seen it first. Just above the tree line in the woods ahead hovered an unclaimed gray Pokémon gym. They had almost walked right past it.

"Wow, good eye," said Sarah.

"Yeah, I'm pretty good at seeing things," Skip agreed.

They rushed over. Sarah was about to suggest that she use her Rattata to claim the gym. She was trying to think of a tactful way to say that her Pokémon seemed pretty tough, and Charlotte's Pidgey had looked a little stringy and weak. But before she could say anything, a great flash of yellow burst forth from the trees and surprised them. It was a Pokémon almost as tall as an eleven-year-old, and stood upright on two legs. It had a long prehensile snout that it could move around, almost like an arm. It was sniffing at the air furiously, twisting around in excitement. Obviously, it had picked up the scent of the incense. As it searched for the source of the wonderful smell, it manipulated its fingers quickly like a gourmet anticipating a wonderful meal.

"A Drowzee!" shouted Skip. "I like them because they're yellow. Which is, of course, the color of the best team."

Charlotte and Sarah both side-eyed Skip.

"It looks pretty strong and healthy," Sarah said, sizing the Pokémon up. "Why don't we catch it, and use *it* to stock the gym?"

"That sounds good to me," said Skip. "Can I do the honors? Pretty-please?"

"He's all yours," Sarah said.

Skip took out a Poké Ball, concentrated on the sniffing Drowzee, and took a deep breath.

"Okay, buddy," Skip said. "Here we go. One throw."

Sarah was not clear about whether Skip was addressing the Pokémon or himself.

Skip hurled the Poké Ball and struck the Drowzee in the middle of its chest. Even as it began to shrink, the beast continued to sniff the air and twiddle its fingers, still confident it would soon find the source of the delicious odor. The Drowzee was sucked into the ball. The ball fell to the ground. It shuddered once . . . twice . . .

And then opened back up!

All at once, the Drowzee reappeared in front of them. Still sniffing. Still curious.

"Darn it!" said Skip.

"See, I told you this one was tougher," said Sarah. "That's not a bad thing. It means that Drowzee will do a better job of holding the gym if we can catch it."

"What do you mean *if*?" said Skip, clearly offended. "I'd say it's more a matter of *when*."

Skip reared back and hurled a second Poké Ball. Again, he struck the Pokémon in the center of the chest. Again it shrank down and was sucked into the ball. The ball fell to the grass and began to vibrate.

"Please, please, please . . ." Skip chanted to himself.

The ball stopped vibrating. There was an audible click. The Pokémon was caught.

"Oh, yes!" said Skip, raising his arms triumphantly over his head. "You got *got*, Mr. Drowzee!"

"I don't know how I feel about *Mr. Drowzee* as a name," said Charlotte. "You're just taking the Pokémon's name and putting *Mr.* in front of it. Also, how do you know that it isn't a girl?"

"Sheesh, I wasn't trying to name it," said Skip, bending over and snatching up the Poké Ball. "I was just, you know, acting happy I caught it."

"I think the best way to celebrate will be to use the Drowzee to stock that gym over there," Sarah urged.

"Sounds good to me," said Skip.

He walked up to the empty gray gym and tossed the Poké Ball containing the Drowzee right into the center. The Drowzee spawned and was teleported to the top of the gym, which soon turned a shade of yellow quite close to that of the Drowzee itself. Skip smiled in satisfaction.

No sooner was this complete than there was another rustling in the bushes nearby. All three kids turned to face it, anticipating another Pokémon. Sarah even readied a Poké Ball. But instead, one of the alien Pokémon trainers emerged. He strode confidently out of the underbrush without so much as saying hello.

"What gives?" Skip said to it. "Have you been watching us? Following us?"

The Pokémon trainer ignored Skip. He moved almost like a zombie or robot, as if Skip wasn't even there.

"How rude," said Charlotte.

Wordlessly, the Pokémon trainer walked over to the gym and opened his backpack, produced a Poké Ball of its own. It tossed the ball at the Pokémon gym where the Drowzee waited. There was a startling sound as the Poké Ball opened to reveal ta creature inside.

"He's trying to take our gym already!" said Charlotte.

As they looked on, the trainer's Pokémon spawned into existence. The creature revealed was similar to the Pidgey that Charlotte had caught. However, as it unfolded its wings they saw that it was much larger. And, most strikingly, it had a shock of bright red feathers piled together at the top of its head, almost like a pompadour haircut.

"It's a Pidgeotto," said Skip. "Wow."

Sarah was more confused than astonished.

"How on earth did the other team already evolve a Pidgeotto?" she asked. "We've only just started playing. To do that, they would have had to have caught four Pidgey already."

"I guess that's technically possible," said Charlotte. "Especially if you had twice as many people catching them."

They looked back at the gym. The Pokémon had squared off. The battle was beginning.

The Drowzee and the Pidgeotto circled each other on the top disc of the gym. The Drowzee began to attack with psychic attacks. Each time it did, it stomped its yellow foot. (Sarah didn't know if feet were involved in psychic attacks, or if the

Drowzee just did this for added emphasis.) The Pidgeotto attacked by swooping down near the Drowzee and flapping its wings violently to throw a current of air so swift that it did damage.

"That's an Air Cutter," Skip observed as they watched the fight. "I sure wouldn't like to be on the other side of one."

The Drowzee began to look unsteady under the constant barrage.

"Uh oh," said Sarah. "I'm not sure I like our chances."

No sooner were these words out of her mouth than a powerful gust of wind blew the Drowzee completely off its feet. It crashed to the floor of the gym, knocked out and defeated. Almost immediately, the color of the gym began to change from yellow to jet black—the color of the alien Pokémon trainer's backpack. The Pidgeotto was teleported to the space right above the top of the gym where it flapped its wings in all its grandeur. A Poké Ball fell out of the gym and landed at Skip's feet. Skip realized it contained his defeated Drowzee. It would need to be revived before it could fight again.

For the first and only time, the alien Pokémon trainer acknowledged the existence of Sarah, Skip, and Charlotte, turning to face them and flashing a single, evil grin. Then he hurried away into the woods, in search of the next Pokémon to catch or gym to conquer. In just a few seconds, it had disappeared entirely.

Charlotte said: "That stinks."

Then a strange voice said: "Well, what did you expect to happen?"

Sarah, Skip, and Charlotte looked back and forth at one another.

"Who said . . ." Sarah began.

"I did," the voice came again.

"Where are you?" Sarah asked. "Who's talking?"

From out of the trees, a shape appeared. It was a pink beast about four feet tall that might have passed for a kind of a dinosaur were it not for its almost supernaturally long tongue—over six feet long—that it seemed capable of extending completely or retracting entirely inside its mouth at will. It was a Lickitung, Sarah realized. Apparently, a very talkative one.

Without hesitating, Skip readied a Poké Ball.

"Wait," said Sarah. "Don't do that."

"Why?" said Skip. "He looks tough. He's probably worth a lot of CP."

"Well, for one, I think he can talk," Sarah said.

She inched closer to the Lickitung. She was well aware she was in range of its long tongue. If it felt like giving her a sloppy lick on the face like a dog, there was nothing she was going to be able to do about it.

"Did you just say something?" she asked.

The Lickitung nodded. "I sure did."

Sarah was momentarily speechless. The Pokémon absently licked the back of its own head while it waited for her to recover.

"But . . . but . . . Pokémon can't talk," Sarah sputtered.

"Except to say their own names or utter battle cries and things," Skip pointed out.

"Yes," Sarah said. "Except for that."

"Oh," said the Lickitung. "Sorry. Nobody told *me* that. I think most Pokémon don't speak because they just don't have the right equipment for it. Some don't even have mouths. I think I got lucky being a Lickitung, because I have a mouth and a tongue . . . even if my tongue is kind of long. Okay, really long. Okay, really, *really* long."

"Back where we come from, Pokémon don't talk *period*," Skip objected. "Even if they have a mouth and a tongue and stuff."

"Are you where you come from?" asked the Lickitung, "or are you some other place?"

Skip smiled. The Lickitung had him there, and he knew it.

"I tried to talk to the last group of players," the Lickitung said.

Sarah realized it meant Richard, and the rest of their friends.

"Just as I was about to tell them something very important, they went and threw a Poké Ball at me. Just like you almost did."

"What important thing could you have to tell them?" asked Sarah. "That you like to lick things a lot. I'm sure they already knew that."

The Lickitung did not look amused. "Here's the thing. There's no way you're going to beat these other Pokémon trainers—these aliens—playing six-on-three. They'll be able to catch more of us Pokémon and evolve us more quickly, and you'll just never be able to keep up."

"But we're really, really good at Pokémon GO," said Sarah. "I don't mean to brag, but we're kind of the best in our world."

"Those guys you're up against are good, too," said the Lickitung. "They're the best *their* world had. Think about it."

Sarah crossed her arms and frowned. This was an unpleasant thought, but she had to admit the Lickitung had a point.

"But you're in luck," continued the Lickitung. "Because I know a way you can win. At least, I think I do."

"Wait, why do you want us to win?" interrupted Skip. "Why do you have an interest in the outcome at all? And also, why should we trust you? What if you're a trap sent by the other team to distract us? We could be wasting valuable Pokémon-catching time talking to you, while they get even further ahead."

"I want you to win because I like the world that you come from," said the Lickitung. "In your world, people are kind to Pokémon. Humans are a kind species, generally. At least . . . compared to *them*. These folks you're playing against are really rotten. I don't like to think what would happen if they came into your world."

"I believe the Lickitung, Skip," said Sarah. "It doesn't feel like it's been sent here to distract or trick us. And it's right. Those other Pokémon trainers are jerks compared to us. Anybody can see that from a mile away."

She turned back to the Pokémon. "Tell us how we can win," she said.

"There is a Pokémon who lives on this island called the Ancient Venomoth," said the Lickitung. "It is old and wise. It knows a lot of things. It is said that it knows a way that all the gyms on this island could easily be taken."

"How?" asked Sarah.

"Well . . . it hasn't said *precisely*," answered the Lickitung. "But most of us suspect this means he knows the location of . . . a Ditto."

There was the sharp sound of inhaled breath from three different sets of lungs.

"I thought they weren't even going to have the Ditto in Pokémon GO," sputtered Skip.

"A Ditto can transform itself into any other Pokémon it wants to," exclaimed Charlotte. "Any Pokémon at all! That would mean . . ."

"That would mean it could transform into whatever Pokémon was best to use against whatever was defending a gym," concluded Sarah. "Even if the Pokémon in the gym had enormous CP or HP, it wouldn't matter. The Ditto could always transform into its greatest weakness."

All three looked back at the Lickitung.

"So the Ancient Venomoth knows where we can find a Ditto?" Sarah asked.

"That's what they say," said the Lickitung. "Why don't you let me take you to the Ancient Venemoth? It's not far."

Sarah thought for a moment. Then she turned around to face the rest of her team.

"Guys, I think we should trust this Lickitung and try," she said. "I know it means taking a risk, but it might be our only shot to win. We're outnumbered, and the other team already knows the island."

"I agree," said Charlotte.

"Yeah," added Skip. "That other team won't be so smug when they see that we're packing an honest-to-goodness Ditto!"

"But I also . . . think I should go alone," said Sarah.

Skip and Charlotte's faces fell.

"What?" said Skip. "But I wanna go, too."

"So do I," added Charlotte. "The Ancient Venomoth sounds interesting. And he sort of has a name, if *Ancient* counts as a name."

"But if we all go to see the Ancient Venomoth, then it will be as though our team stopped playing," said Sarah. "The other Pokémon trainers might take all the gyms, and then we lose. While I go with the Lickitung, I need both of you to hold as many gyms as you can. Keep the other team at bay until I get back."

She turned to the Lickitung. "How long will this take?"

The Lickitung shrugged.

"The Ancient Venomoth isn't far," it said. "How long it takes you to convince it to tell you its secret is another matter."

She turned back to Skip and Charlotte. "Can you guys do this? Can you keep fighting for gyms until I return with the Ditto?"

Skip and Charlotte looked disappointed they wouldn't be coming along, but they both nodded in agreement. Each realized what was at stake. Meeting an Ancient Venomoth might be fun, but winning the contest was far more important.

"Great," said Sarah. "I know you'll both do your best until I return."

"Ready to go?" asked the Lickitung.

"Yes," said Sarah. "Let's not waste any more time."

The Lickitung turned around and began to shuffle back into the woods. (Lickitungs are not graceful walkers.) Sarah followed after it. She was excited at the chance to capture a Ditto. She also had absolutely zero idea of how to convince a Venomoth to tell her where one was. She would have to make this up as she went along.

Skip and Charlotte watched Sarah and the Lickitung leave. When Sarah and the Lickitung were out of sight, they turned back to the black gym with the Pidgeotto inside, determined to retake it.

PART SIX

"**N**ot much farther," said the Lickitung excitedly. "Not much farther at all. The Venomoth lives in a cave along the edge of the island. It's very close."

Sarah followed the Lickitung through the trees. She hoped it knew where it was going, because they took so many twists and turns that she was quickly disoriented.

They emerged from the tree line and walked out onto the rocky coast. This was the first time since the start of the contest that Sarah had seen beyond the island. When she turned and gazed westward, back in the direction of her home, she saw something strange—a house was certainly there, but it was both hers and not hers. It looked as though the house where she lived had been merged with another house—a house from another dimension. The two were stuck together and somehow blended. The other house had terrifying spikes along the roof like the back of a dinosaur, and ugly archways that made Sarah think of a giant empty whale skeleton.

The Lickitung glanced over its shoulder and saw that Sarah was momentarily transfixed. "While you have your contest, this island sits in two place at once," the it said.

"Yeah, I think I got that. I also think the other place looks scary. I don't think I'd like it very much."

"I agree," the Lickitung told her. "And that's why I want to make sure your team wins."

The Lickitung led Sarah along the edge of the beach until they reached a small inlet with a tiny cave. "That's where we're going," it said.

The walls of the cave were slippery with green lichen. And it smelled . . . odd. Sarah didn't know how Ancient Venomoth smelled, but this felt about right. The Lickitung barely fit inside. Sarah had to stoop.

They encountered what appeared to be circular waist-high boulders covered with hairy moss. Then one of them moved. Sarah turned on her phone and used its glowing face as a flashlight. She quickly realized that these hairy boulders were Venonat.

"This is where they live during the day," said the Lickitung. "So far, no Pokémon players have discovered this cave. If they did, it would be a cinch to catch a bunch of these guys and quickly evolve a Venomoth. There must be a hundred down here."

Sarah thought the Lickitung was probably not exaggerating.

"Keep up," said the Lickitung. "The Ancient Venomoth is just ahead."

And it was.

They rounded a bend in the cavern corridor and were confronted with a majestic throne carved all out of rock. Upon it sat the Ancient Venomoth in all of its glory. It was slightly larger than Sarah, and looked as though its flying days might be long over. *Ancient* was truly the right word. Its enormous wings were wrinkly and frayed at the tips, and its large eyes were slightly clouded over. Yet, despite all this, it exuded a mightiness that Sarah could not doubt. If it wanted to, it could still prove a very powerful adversary. Sarah wondered how many CP it had. She reckoned it must be well into the four figures.

The Venomoth raised its hoary head and slowly looked back and forth between Sarah and the Lickitung. When it spoke, it's voice was a like a strange and ancient buzz. "You again?"

Sarah realized it was addressing the Lickitung.

"Yes," said the Lickitung. "I'm back because I have found someone who can solve your problem."

The Ancient Venomoth looked at Sarah skeptically. If it had worn glasses, Sarah felt sure it would have looked over the top of them at her.

"*This* person is going solve our problem?" asked the Ancient Venomoth skeptically.

"This is one of the players," said the Lickitung. "She is the very best on her team. Probably in the entire contest."

A wave of alarm rippled through the Venonat who surrounded their leader. The shaggy globes jiggled nervously. A few rushed forward to block Sarah's line of sight.

"And you brought her here? What were you thinking?"

"Just listen to me," pleaded the Lickitung. "Remember that problem you were telling me about? The one with the Seel? I think she can help!"

The Ancient Venomoth looked suspicious. "She's not here to try and catch us? Because, I assure you, I am *very hard* to catch."

"Nothing like that," said the Lickitung. "See? She didn't catch me, did she?"

"Very well," said the Ancient Venomoth. It still did not sound entirely satisfied.

Sarah stepped forward. The Venonat shuffled nervously. "What is it that you need help with, exactly?" she asked.

"First of all, we do not, in any sense, *need help*," the Ancient Venomoth said sternly. "We are perfectly happy here inside our cave. Isn't that right?"

The Venonat vibrated in agreement.

"However, I suppose it would be nice if someone happened to clean up all of the Seel who have colonized this coast of the island."

"What's wrong with the Seel?" asked Sarah.

"They take up all the good real estate," said the Ancient Venomoth. "They always bother us and try to push us around. Of course, I'm strong and mighty. There's not a Seel or a Dewgong I can't face down. But . . . I can't be everywhere at once, can I? The poor Venonat are always getting the short end of the stick."

"That's odd," Sarah replied.

"What is?" asked the Ancient Venomoth.

"Well, it's just that I always thought Seel would be pleasant and friendly, like the seals in the world where I come from," she replied. "True, I haven't met any actual Pokémon until recently, but I guess I thought I'd be able to guess their temperaments."

"Perhaps the seals of your world aren't a bunch of beach-hogging jerks, but I can't say the same is true here."

"So you'd like me to clear them out for you?" asked Sarah.

"Yes, that would be agreeable," pronounced the Venomoth.

Suddenly, the Lickitung spoke up. "And if she does this for you, I believe that you ought to do a favor for her. They say you know the location of a . . . Let's say, a thing that would make it easy for any Pokémon trainer to win all of the gyms on this island."

"It is true that I have this knowledge," said the Ancient Venomoth cagily.

"Then you should share it with her if she does this favor for you," insisted the Lickitung.

The Ancient Venomoth stretched its wings and adjusted itself, considering.

"As you wish," it eventually said.

The Lickitung looked at Sarah excitedly.

"Well, thanks very much," Sarah said brightly to the Venomoth. "I'll go have a word with those Seel, and be back before you know it."

The Ancient Venomoth shrugged, as though it was not particularly excited about the outcome either way. Sarah made her way out of the cave, and the Lickitung followed. Back on the beach, it took her only a moment to spot her first Seel.

"There's one!" she cried. "I'm going to get to work!"

"Sounds good to me," said the Lickitung. "I'll probably sit here on the beach and watch. This has already involved a lot more walking than I'm used to."

"You're *tired*?" Sarah asked. She felt more energized than she'd ever been before.

"You just try walking around all over the place with a tongue that weighs half as much as you do," the Lickitung said. "It'll tire you out."

"Fine, but while you're just sitting there, how about keeping an eye out for Seel? Telling me where you see one? That kind of thing . . ."

"I can do that," said the Lickitung, settling itself on top of the beach's largest, highest rock.

Sarah took a Poké Ball from out of her backpack and began stalking the Seel, which was frolicking in the water a few yards down the beach.

"Watch where you throw that thing," the Lickitung called after her.

"Yeah, yeah," said Sarah. "If I'd wanted to catch you, I would have already."

"I might be craftier than you think," the Lickitung called back.

Sarah reached the Seel. She could already see two other Seel and a Dewgong playing farther down the beach. The Ancient Venomoth was right. They *did* kind of cluster together and take up all the good real estate.

"You're coming with me," Sarah cried as she took aim and launched her Poké Ball at the Seel. It lounged like a fat sunbather and looked up at the last moment as the ball careened off its belly and popped open. The surprised Seel shrank in size and sucked into the ball. The Poké Ball tumbled to the ground and fell still. Sarah picked it up and deposited it safely in her backpack.

Looking up the beach, she saw that the other Seel, and even the Dewgong, had noticed her. A moment later, another pair of Seel emerged from the water and joined them. How many Seel were on this beach anyway? Sarah rolled up her sleeves. She was going to find out.

Twenty minutes later—though it felt like a small eternity had passed—Sarah stomped back up the beach to where the Lickitung was sunning itself on the rock. She had captured fifteen Seel and five Dewgong, and used exactly twenty Poké Balls. Not a single one of them had eluded Sarah's perfect throws. She was sweaty and her arm was starting to get sore, but she had captured all of them.

"You didn't help at *all*," she shouted to the Lickitung. "You were supposed to at least help me look for Seel."

"It seemed like you had it under control," said the Lickitung. "Also, I got distracted keeping an eye on something else."

"Sure you did," said Sarah skeptically.

"Don't believe me?" replied the Lickitung. "Here, stand on my rock. But don't look out. Look in, toward at the island."

The Lickitung hopped off its rock, and motioned for Sarah to take a turn standing on it. She didn't know what the Pokémon was talking about, but decided to humor it. She pulled herself up to the top of the rock and looked.

"My goodness," she said. "There's a great view from up here. I think I can see all of the PokéStops on the island, and all of the gyms, too."

"It's the ones in the second category that've caught my attention," said the Lickitung.

Sarah looked more closely at the gyms. She counted all ten of them. Each gym was now occupied, and featured a Pokémon slowly rotating at the top. Each also featured a color. When Sarah recounted to make sure, she realized that only two gyms were yellow, and only one was red.

"Oh no," said Sarah. "This means that Skip and Charlotte have only been able to control three gyms. And the bad guys already control seven!"

As Sarah looked on, she saw smoke and flame beginning to rise from one of the yellow gyms—a telltale sign that the gym was being fought over.

"We may be down to two before long." Sarah said. "I need to get this Ditto as quickly as possible, and then get back to the fight!"

"Sounds good to me," said the Lickitung.

Sarah leapt down off of the tall rock and headed back along the coastline until she arrived back at the cave of the Ancient Venomoth. She ducked inside, picking her way past the curious Venonat that lined the corridor. Behind her, the Lickitung huffed and puffed, struggling to keep up.

"Are you coming or not?" Sarah called behind her.

"Yes, I'm coming," the Lickitung wheezed. "Do I need to remind you that I'm mostly tongue? Sheesh."

They arrived in front of the Ancient Venomoth. Its eyes appeared to be lidless, and it may have been sleeping. It stretched itself awake as Sarah presented herself.

"Back so soon?" it buzzed.

"I am," said Sarah. "And I'm pleased to announce that the beachfront property is all yours. That is to say, its free from Seel and Dewgong."

"It . . . It . . ." Sarah and the Ancient Venomoth looked back down the corridor to where the Lickitung struggled to jog and talk at the same time. "It's true," the Lickitung said. "She caught every last one."

Sarah opened her backpack and approached the Ancient Venomoth. She held the open backpack below its hornlike nose so it could see all of the filled Poké Balls.

"Hmm," said the Ancient Venomoth. "I believe in your world they have a saying: "Trust but verify." I believe my Venonat can make that happen."

At this, several furry orbs sprang up and ran out of the cave. Moments later, they returned. Vibrating, they nodded up and down, confirming Sarah had indeed cleared the beach.

"Very well," said the Ancient Venomoth. "I thank you for providing this service to us. Now, what was it you wanted in return?"

"The Lickitung said you know of something that can help me take all of the gyms on this island," Sarah replied. "We're in a contest right now with some very bad people. We need to defeat them. I really need to take these gyms and time is running out."

The Ancient Venomoth looked down at Sarah.

"My dear," it said in a grandfatherly way, "you already have everything you need to win the contest. There is nothing more I can give you."

Sarah was shocked.

"Excuse me," she said. "Did I hear you right? Because that sure sounded like you're not going to tell me what I need to know. Even after all I just did for you?"

The Ancient Venomoth did not move or speak.

"Well . . . that's just . . . *rude*," Sarah sputtered. "I can't believe this!"

She turned and marched out of the cave. "You're lucky I don't catch you all right now," she called as she stomped away.

Sarah found herself back on the newly Seel-free beach. She turned inland and headed into the woods, angry and determined. A few steps in the trees, she heard a familiar voice behind her.

"Wait," the Lickitung called. "Where are you going?"

"Where do you *think* I'm going?" Sarah said. "We're down to three gyms. Maybe fewer by now. I'm going to find Skip and Charlotte and try to win this contest before it's too late!"

"But . . ." sputtered the Lickitung.

"Stop bothering me!" Sarah shouted in frustration. "I just lost a bunch of time I could have spent catching Pokémon. I'm starting to wonder if the other team didn't put you up to this! Whose side are you on, anyway?"

"*Your* side!" said the Lickitung. "Honestly, I thought he would tell you where to find the Ditto. Really, I did!"

"From now on, maybe you should keep your thoughts to yourself," Sarah said as she stalked away.

Sarah made her way toward the nearest Pokémon gym. It was black, and controlled by the other team, but she could see that someone was battling for it. The Sandshrew that held it was putting up a powerful fight against some unseen force.

The gym was located in a clearing where a tiny stream flowed. Stepping into the clearing, Sarah saw both Skip and Charlotte. They looked exhausted, but also determined to put up the fight of their lives. Skip had fed a Bulbasaur into the gym to fight the Sandshrew. Charlotte was busy stacking a group of filled Poké Balls together. For a moment, Sarah was unclear about exactly what Charlotte was doing. Then the balls began to glow. One of them opened and a Paras emerged. It began to float in the air. The Paras looked as surprised as anyone by this. Its bug eyes went wide and its sideways mouth opened in alarm. The Paras floated about ten feet into the sky, and there was a tremendous flash. The Paras was not there any longer—it had been replaced by a Parasect with great, crablike claws and a large mushroom hat. The Parasect floated back down and into a single Poké Ball. All of the other balls had disappeared in the flash. Sarah realized that Charlotte was evolving Pokémon.

Just as Charlotte finished this, Skip's Bulbasaur was defeated by the Sandshrew.

"Dang it!" Skip cried in frustration.

"Here," Charlotte said. "Try this."

She tossed Skip the PokéBall containing the Parasect. Skip lobbed it into the gym. The Parasect spawned and went right to work attacking the Sandshrew.

Charlotte and Skip noticed Sarah standing at the edge of the clearing. They tore themselves away from the combat and hurried over to her.

"Omigosh!" Charlotte said. "Thank goodness you're here!"

"Yeah," said Skip. "Taking over these gyms is really hard. We take a gym, and then the other team takes it right back. We can never seem to catch enough Pokémon to keep up with them."

"Did you get the Ditto?" Charlotte asked.

Both Skip and Charlotte could see from the expression on Sarah's face that the answer was no.

"The Lickitung was right about there being an Ancient Venomoth who needed a favor. I caught a whole beach full of Seel for it. But then when I asked for the reward, he didn't give it to me."

"That's outrageous . . . and not in a good way," said Sarah.

"He just said no?" asked Skip.

"He acted like I didn't need it," said Sarah. "He said I already had everything I needed to win."

"Gee, what a bum," said Skip.

Charlotte, however, looked thoughtful, carefully considering what Sarah had just said.

"What?" asked Sarah. "What is it?"

"Oh," said Charlotte. "I was just wondering if he could have meant the Seel. Like maybe the reward for catching the Seel *was* the Seel."

"No, no," said Sarah. "I suppose we could use them to evolve some good Dewgong, but not enough to take over the whole island."

"Maybe you ought to give that a shot anyway," suggested Charlotte. "At this point, we need to try everything we can."

"Okay," said Sarah. "If you think it'll help."

Sarah emptied all of the Seel Poké Balls from her backpack and began stacking them together as she had seen Charlotte do. Soon, she had evolved several mighty Dewgong that looked like they would be a real force to be reckoned with. Still, Sarah knew they were not powerful enough to be able to take over every gym on the island.

"Wow," said Skip. "Those look great."

"They are pretty tough," Sarah agreed. "I'm just not certain they'll be enough to turn the tide in the contest."

Just as those words were out of her mouth, there was a flash, and a change of color in the gym behind them. The Parasect had defeated the Sandshrew.

"Nice!" said Skip. "Thanks for evolving that, Charlotte."

"Happy to help," she said.

"I've got an idea," Skip added. "Let's throw one of those big Dewgong in there to help the Parasect hold the gym. Like an added anchor."

"Okay," said Sarah.

She tossed one of her Poké Balls containing a Dewgong into the gym. It floated up and took its place beside the Parasect. Sarah decided her brother was right. It looked like it would be able to hold the gym for a while.

No sooner had Sarah done this than a Pokémon trainer from the other team walked into the clearing. The Pokémon trainer was smiling confidently, but the smile fell from her face when she saw the mighty Dewgong. It was clear she understood that taking *this* gym back was going to be quite a challenge.

"C'mon," said Charlotte, tugging at Sarah's sleeve. "We need to hurry to the next gym. We don't have time to hang around and watch. This is how it works. Because we're outnumbered, we're always going to have to run."

"At least that Dewgong will hold for a while," said Skip. "Nice going, sis."

They sprinted across the island to the next nearest gym. Skip and Charlotte seemed to have memorized where they were. Sarah was thankful, at least, for that.

This next gym was purple, and was being held by a bright green Scyther. It hovered up and down on enormous wings. From time to time, it swung its sharp, powerful arms. It didn't have its

CP displayed, but Sarah could tell it was mighty indeed.

"Gee," said Charlotte. "That guy looks really tough. I don't think I have a Pokémon that can defeat it."

"I don't think I do, either," said Skip. "Do you want to just go on to the next gym?"

"Wait," called Sarah. "What about one of my evolved Dewgong? Could that do the job?"

"It's worth a shot," Charlotte said. "We don't have anything else nearly as powerful."

Sarah approached the gym where the enormous Scyther hovered. It looked down at her and flexed its arms like an athlete preparing for a contest. It seemed to know it was about to be challenged.

Sarah tossed the Poké Ball containing her mightiest Dewgong into the center of the gym. She watched excitedly as it opened and the familiar looking water-type Pokémon emerged. The two beasts were soon locked in combat. Sarah held her breath. If this Pokémon didn't take the gym, they had no plan B.

The Dewgong began attacking with its frost breath weapon. The Scyther countered with Fury Cutter, which seemed to startle the Dewgong. Then, while it was dazed, the Scyther hit it with a concentrated X-Scissor. The Dewgong was clearly hurting now. It continued to attack, but it didn't look as though it would last long. The Scyther, on the other hand, seemed like it could battle all day. Like it was gaining strength and confidence with each passing moment. The Dewgong went to launch an Aqua Jet, but the Scyther hit it once more with the X-Scissor. The Dewgong was done for. Completely knocked out, it fell to the gym floor in an undignified heap. The Poké Ball sucked it back inside, and then fell out of the gym and landed on the grass below. The Scyther returned to its position in the air above the gym, glowering down and gloating, or so it seemed to Sarah.

"*Ugh*," said Charlotte. "I thought for sure that Dewgong would do the trick."

"I did not expect that Scyther to be so strong," said Skip. "Just goes to show you."

Sarah didn't say anything. She'd sat down on the ground in front of the gym and was weeping.

"Sarah . . ." Charlotte called to her. "Hey. It's not that bad."

"Yes it is," Sarah said between sobs. "It is *too* that bad."

Skip seemed a ambivalent about how to react to this development. Frequently when his sister was reduced to tears, it was because she had been successfully defeated in some way that favored *him*.

His natural reaction was to be pleased with any situation in which Sarah bawled. But today they were on the same team, and there was a lot at stake. Skip threw his regular playbook out the window.

"Sis, is there . . . err . . . anything I can do to help you feel better?" he asked awkwardly, like someone speaking in a foreign language for the first time.

Sarah did not respond.

"We can't just sit down and give up, Sarah," urged Charlotte. "We've *got* to keep playing. Sure, we lost this fight, but there will be others. Maybe the next gym will have a tiny Weedle inside and will be easy to take."

"No it won't!" Sarah roared. It was clear that she had had enough. "I'm sick of how unfair this game is!" she continued. "I wasn't sure about playing in the first place. But playing against a team of twice as many players, and they already know the island? This stinks! I wish we'd never come here. I wish my mom hadn't inherited that stupid house with the stupid island behind it. I wish I'd never met Alice. I wish I'd never caught that stupid Charmander. I wish I'd never seen a real Poké Ball. I wish—"

"Sarah!" interrupted Charlotte. "What did you just say?"

Sarah paused for a moment and wiped at her eyes.

"I said I wish I never saw a real Poké Ball."

"*Before* that!" urged Charlotte.

"I . . . uh . . . I wish I had never caught that Charmander?" Sarah tried.

Charlotte waived her hands dramatically as if this meant something vitally important. Sarah didn't quite see what could be so important about it.

"You caught that Charmander with a Poké Ball," Charlotte said, like a teacher trying to help a student hit upon an answer.

"Well duh," said Sarah. "Of course I did. How else would you expect me to catch it?"

"So then you still have it?"

Sarah thought for a moment. She'd brought the Poké Ball with her, and had almost certainly added it to the other Poké Balls inside her backpack. She couldn't precisely remember. She took off her backpack and rooted inside until she had, indeed, located the Poké Ball in question. She pulled it out and tossed it to Charlotte.

"There you go. To tell you the truth, I'd forgotten all about it. But why do you bring it up now? The Charmander inside's not going to be any match for that Scyther. Now, a Charizard on the other hand . . ."

Charlotte accepted the Poké Ball, but seemed undeterred.

"Sarah, that Ancient Venomoth you went and talked to . . . It told you that you already had everything you needed to win, right?"

"That's right," said Sarah. "But that doesn't help me. I was hoping he was going to tell me where to find a Ditto. That's what the Lickitung thought he would do."

"Sarah, don't you see?" said Charlotte. "What if he told you that because you already *had* the Ditto?"

"But how could I—"

Sarah stopped herself. She didn't need to say the rest out loud. The Charmander. She had always assumed that it was, well, a Charmander. Because it couldn't be anything other than itself, right?

Except now, maybe it could.

Sarah realized that the Pokémon she'd captured with an almost-accidental terror-throw along the beach might actually be something completely different from what she'd thought. And it could also be the answer they were looking for.

"Here," Charlotte said, handing the Poké Ball back to Sarah. "It's yours. Maybe you should do the honors?"

"Okay," said Sarah. She wiped the last of the tears from her face and took the Poké Ball. She stalked over to the gym. Above her, the Scyther still hovered, regarding them with a confident smile.

Sarah tossed the Poké Ball into the gym. It opened and a familiar-looking Charmander emerged. The flat floor of the gym spread out and the Scyther floated down, ready to fight. Sarah knew she only had moments to act. Here went nothing.

"Ditto!" Sarah called as loudly as she could. "Take the form of a Snorlax. A very *large* Snorlax who specializes in Body Slam!"

The Charmander turned and looked at her. The Scyther looked, too. (It had probably never heard a Pokémon player give commands like that before.) Then a remarkable thing happened. The Charmander began to grow large and wide, as though it were a balloon being blown up. Its color changed from reddish-brown to blue and white. Its ears retracted to two tiny points, and its teeth came and went until only two prominent canine teeth were showing on the bottom. The Pokémon bounced up and down a couple of times, then turned around to face its opponent.

It was indeed now a Snorlax. The mightiest Snorlax that Sarah, or any of the others, had ever seen. (It was also, apparently, the largest Snorlax that the Scyther had ever seen. The Scyther did not have eyebrows *per se*, but still managed to use its eyes to get across the fact that it was very, *very* surprised by what it was seeing.)

The combat began.

The Snorlax began peppering the Scyther with a series of powerful head butts. The Scyther was a bit dazed, but still managed to stay upright. However, as it fought, the Snorlax seemed to grow more and more confident. It was almost as if it were building to something.

As it turned out, it was.

After dodging a couple of the Scyther's counter attacks, the Snorlax went into its signature move, the Body Slam. There were many Pokémon that used Body Slam as a special attack, but none of these Pokémon were as large as a Snorlax. And since Body Slam involved literally slamming down your body on top of an opponent, overall mass counted for a whole lot. The Scyther was about to find that out the hard way.

The Scyther sensed what was happening a moment too late. It tried to take evasive action and jump to the side, but it wasn't quick enough. The Snorlax descended with the thunder of a mountain. The entire gym (and even the ground beneath it) seemed to shake under the Snorlax's weight. The enormous Pokémon rolled off of the Scyther and got back up very slowly. The Scyther underneath it had been smashed almost perfectly flat.

"Holy cats," said Charlotte. "It worked."

"Niiiiiiice," said Skip. "Take that, you stupid Scyther."

"This changes everything," said Sarah, bewildered and pleased all at once. "Now we need to hold this gym and use the Ditto to take the others and quickly as we can. I'll use another of the Dewgong."

Sarah tossed a Poké Ball containing a Dewgong into the gym and removed the Ditto.

"Sweet," said Skip as the gym turned blue and the Dewgong began rotating happily above them. "I feel like we just got a second wind."

"Yeah," said Sarah. "Let's not waste it."

And with that, they hurried off across the island.

PART SEVEN

The next gym controlled by the opposing team was along the coast. It had turned orange and featured a nasty looking Pokémon made out of a string of rocks that became progressively larger as they neared the creature's head. Its eyes were narrow and it had one long spike protruding from its forehead. It thrashed back and forth, ready for action.

"Hmm, looks like an Onix," said Sarah. "How do we want to play this?"

"A Lapras can do lots of damage against rock-type Pokémon," Charlotte said.

"A Lapras can do lots of damage against *anybody*," Skip pointed out.

"Sounds good to me," said Sarah. "Lapras, it is."

Sarah took the Poké Ball containing the Ditto and lobbed it up into the gym. It opened, and the Pokémon emerged in Snorlax form. It bounced up and down, looking for the next opponent to smash.

"Ditto," Sarah called. "Take the form of a Lapras!"

The Ditto obeyed. The Snorlax fell forward onto its belly. Its limbs began to elongate and thicken until they resembled the paddles of a plesiosaur. The back of the Snorlax hardened into a crusty shell. Its ears morphed into a pair of tightly curled horns. It took on a blue skin tone with a bright white underbelly.

The Ditto turned and looked back at Sarah, as if to confirm that it was ready for action.

"Woo!" Skip shouted with excitement. "Go Lapras! I mean, Ditto!"

"I'll cheer for anybody as long as they're on our team," added Charlotte.

The Lapras and the Onix began to fight. The Onix struck first, attacking with Rock Throw. It hurdled rocks across the gym at the Lapras. (Whether the rocks were part of itself or were magically generated was a point on which Sarah was never completely clear. The important thing was that the Onix sure seemed to have a lot of them.) The Lapras did its best to move out of the way, but it made a massive target and was easy for the Onix to hit. On the other hand, the Onix's attacks seemed to do very little damage.

Then the Lapras found its footing and began to counterattack. It began by blasting the Onix with its frost breath. Right away, it was clear that Charlotte had made the correct suggestion. The Onix was staggered and its health began to fall rapidly.

"Hit it with Ice Beam!" called Skip. "It'll go down with one blast, I bet."

The Lapras must have been thinking along the same lines. It opened its mighty mouth and spewed forth a powerful beam of pure ice. The beam struck the Onix squarely on the forehead. The Onix looked up at its own horn for a moment—the very spot the beam had connected—and then its eyes gradually began to cross. It slowly deflated and fell to the floor of the gym. It curled and went flat until it looked like an old gray sock. It had been knocked out.

"Yes!" said Skip. "I knew Ice Beam would work."

"I think we all knew Ice Beam would work against an Onix," Charlotte pointed out.

"Okay, but I'm the one who told the Ditto to use it," Skip said, his sense of superiority quite obviously still intact.

"I'm going to do what we did the last time and secure the gym with a Dewgong," said Sarah. She fed one of the Poké Balls containing a Dewgong into the gym, and carefully extracted the Ditto. The gym turned a healthy shade of blue and the Dewgong was soon rotating above it.

"Nice," said Skip. "I'm starting to think this is actually going to work."

"I am, too," Sarah agreed. "But now I think it's time for us to split up again."

"Huh?" said Skip. "But we're doing great like this!"

"I know," said Sarah, "but keep in mind that to win we need to control all *ten* of the island's gyms. If you and Charlotte can check on some other gyms—or maybe help battle for any that the other team is trying to retake—then I think we can win much more quickly."

"Okay," said Skip. "I guess that makes sense."

"We'll catch back up with you as soon as we can," added Charlotte.

Sarah remained optimistic as she made her way to the next gym. Now that she had a Ditto, it seemed that nothing could stop her! She felt sure that it would only be a matter of time before her team had won the competition.

The results at the next gym did nothing to change Sarah's mind. This gym was colored purple and held by a dangerous looking Bellsprout. (*Well*, thought Sarah, *it looks as dangerous as a surprised yellow flower can reasonably hope to look.*) Sarah knew that Bellsprout spat dangerous acid with great effectiveness, but they were vulnerable to bug-type Pokémon. With this in mind, she morphed the Ditto into a Beedrill. It attacked the Bellsprout viciously with jabs from its conical arms, and launched dazzling charges with its stinger. Before long the Bellsprout was flat on its stem, and the Beedrill/Ditto was victorious.

Just as Sarah finished removing the Ditto from the gym and replacing it with a Dewgong, Charlotte and Skip reemerged from the woods. They both had confused looks on their faces. Sarah wondered what was going on.

"What are you guys doing here?" she asked. "You haven't taken all of the other gyms yet, have you? I think we'd know if the contest was over."

Skip and Charlotte shook their heads.

"Something very strange is happening," said Charlotte.

"We *do* control all of the gyms now . . . except for one," Skip added mysteriously.

"What're you talking about?" Sarah asked.

"We went to check on the gyms, but the other team had left them undefended," Skip said. "Like, empty. We put Pokémon in all of them. With this one you just took, we've got nine out of ten."

"But it gets weirder," Charlotte reported. "All of the Pokémon trainers on the other team have huddled around a single gym. They've filled it with all of their best Pokémon. And now they're searching a particular section of trees beside it."

"That is very odd," said Sarah. "Show me." She followed Skip and Charlotte to the eastern-most edge of the island facing the open sea. As she walked along, Sarah noticed that every gym she passed was now, indeed, red, blue, or yellow. Her team seemed to have taken all but one of the gyms. Then she spotted her destination up ahead—a green gym with a very grumpy looking Gengar rotating in the air above it. The gym appeared to be stocked with three Pokémon total. Sarah thought the Gengar looked tough, but it wouldn't be a problem for her Ditto.

As Charlotte had said, all of the opposing team—all six Pokémon trainers—were searching through the woods beside the gym. They had all activated their incense. Sarah would have remarked on how awesome it smelled . . . if she wasn't so confused.

"What *are* they doing?" Charlotte asked.

"You expect *me* to know?" said Sarah. "I just got here. Let me think."

"We could try asking them," Skip suggested.

He turned to face the Pokémon trainers who stalked intently through the woods. "Hey, why are you guys acting so weird?!" Skip shouted.

A couple of the Pokémon trainers looked over at Skip, but none of them answered.

"Well, I tried," Skip said playfully.

"I just don't see why they're so interested in those woods," Charlotte said. "And why they've given up on all of the other gyms. It just doesn't make sense."

"Except it does."

It was Sarah who had spoken. Something had just become startlingly clear to her. "We've got to take this final gym, and we've got to take it fast!" she added urgently.

"Why?" Charlotte said. "What's going on?"

"They've realized we have a Ditto," said Sarah as she took off her backpack and began rifling through the Poké Balls inside. "What would you do if *you* realized the other team had a Ditto?"

"Honestly, I'd want to give up," said Charlotte. "There'd be no way to win unless you—"

"—caught your own Ditto," Skip finished.

Sarah nodded. "I don't know if they have special knowledge of where you can catch here. Maybe one of them saw a Ditto there during their first contest against Richard, Sammy, and Maria. All I know is that's *got* to be what they're up to. And we need to take this gym before they succeed."

Sarah rushed over to the green gym and tossed in the Poké Ball containing her Ditto. It sprang out as a Beedrill. If it was going to face a Gengar effectively, Sarah wanted a Ditto with Dark attacks. She commanded it to take the form of a Weezing that could attack with Dark Pulse. As everyone looked on intently—including a few of the rival team members—the Beedrill morphed into a Weezing with several floating connected heads and a gaseous mist surrounding it. Sarah tried not to breathe in any of the foul stench. The Weezing squared off against the Gengar and the two Pokémon sized up one another. Then they began to fight.

The Weezing struck first with acid attacks. They seemed to do little more than startle the Gengar. Then the Weezing built up to a Dark Pulse and launched it at full strength. The Gengar shook violently, then the knees on its tiny legs went weak, and it fell straight to the mat. It did not get up again.

"One down, two to go," Sarah said excitedly.

"That was easy enough," said Skip.

"Shh," cautioned Charlotte. "Don't jinx us."

The unconscious Gengar shrank down in size and beamed itself back to the inventory of the opposing Pokémon trainer who had first caught it. Another Pokémon appeared to take its place. It had a body like a brown bean, a sideways mouth that ran vertical instead of horizontal, and angry-looking eyes. Two spiky horns protruded from either side of its forehead.

"Ick, a Pinsir," said Sarah. "*Nobody* likes Pinsir. It will be a pleasure to beat *you*. Ditto, take the form of a Magmar."

The Ditto nodded enthusiastically and began to shed its Weezing form. The floating circular heads morphed together and merged into a body that looked like a heavy metal duck on fire. Great plumes of flame shot from its arms and head. It had long nails, and wore cool-looking black ankle bands and a black collar.

Sarah knew that a Magmar's fire attacks would be especially effective against the Pinsir.

The Pinsir lashed out at the fully-formed Magmar, using its disturbing mouth and giant horns. The Magmar fought back with karate chops, which looked all the more dramatic since they were delivered by flaming wings. The Magmar's hands had spikes along the edges, and these did additional damage, cracking right through the Pinsir's tough insect exoskeleton. When it had built up enough energy from landing karate chops, the Magmar jumped away by doing a dramatic backflip. The Pinsir poked at the air, then hesitated, confused by this tactic. Then all became clear—the Magmar was preparing for a Fire Blast. Before the Pinsir knew what had hit it, it was all over. The Magmar launched a mighty wall of flame in the bug's direction. The Magmar was singed so deeply that it turned entirely black, except for its eyes, which no longer looked menacing at all. Very slowly, the blackened bean fell over.

"Good riddance," Sarah called. "I'm glad to be done with you."

Then the final Pokémon defending the gym stepped into the ring. Everyone held their breath. Everyone, that is, except for Sarah, who was already using her breath to say: "Ditto! Take the form of a Dragonite!"

The Ditto began to evolve into a giant orange dragon with wings and antennae.

The final Pokémon it would face was a Vileplume. Though it looked like a happy blue ball in a fanciful red flower hat, it was a formidable foe. It could attack with a pungent poison capable of incapacitating even the strongest Pokémon if they were exposed to enough of it. That was why Sarah had gone for the big guns. And Dragonite was the biggest gun she knew of. The toughest of tough Pokémon.

Immediately, the Dragonite went to work against the Vileplume with a series of powerful

Dragon Breath attacks. The Vileplume did its best to strike back with dangerous poison sprays, but Sarah knew it would be too little, too late. The Dragonite was building toward a Dragon Pulse. Sarah knew that when it hit, the the contest would be over.

Just as Sarah began to savor the taste of victory, Skip cried out, "Sarah, look!"

She saw him gesture in the direction of the Pokémon trainers. Following his gaze, she saw that the six competitors looked very excited. They were jumping up and down grinning. Sarah didn't like this development at all.

"What's going on," called Charlotte. "What are those guys so happy about?"

"There's only one thing it can be," Sarah said icily.

No sooner were the words out of her mouth than a Pokémon trainer came running over to the gym. As the Dragonite continued to pound away on the poor Vileplume, the Pokémon trainer tossed a single red and white Poké Ball into the gym. At the same moment, the Dragonite launched a devastating Dragon Pulse and knocked out the Vileplume. Its floppy hat of petals carried it softly and slowly down to the mat like a parachute.

"Did it work?" Skip asked. "Have we won?"

"No," said Sarah. "Look. They added another Pokémon just in time."

As the Vileplume faded away, yet another Pokémon walked out onto the central disc of the gym floor. It was a pink, amorphous blob with two tiny pinprick eyes and a very wide slit mouth—a Ditto in its native form.

As Sarah looked on, the opposing Pokémon trainer said something she could not quite hear. Moments later, the Ditto morphed into a Dragonite exactly like the one already in the gym.

"Oh no," said Skip. "They've got a Dragonite, too! It's going to be a Dragonite-on-Dragonite contest. That only gives us a fifty percent chance of winning."

"That is, unless we switch to a different Pokémon," said Charlotte. "But what's better than a Dragonite? Do you know of anything, Sarah? Sarah?"

Sarah didn't respond. She was thinking about what to do. Dragonites certainly had weaknesses, but those were few and far between. Moreover, Dragonites were the mightiest and toughest Pokémon around. Sarah was having trouble thinking of a solution. Meanwhile, the Dragonites were preparing to start their fight.

Then Sarah had an idea. She didn't have time to mull it over, but she decided to just go with it. The idea felt right.

Sarah approached the gym and whispered something to her Ditto. It looked at her with a strange expression. Sarah nodded vigorously to tell the Ditto that it *had* heard her correctly. The Ditto turned back to face its opponent and began to morph. Moments later, it was clear which form it would become . . . a Dewgong!

"What?" exclaimed Skip. "Sis, what did you just do?"

"A Dewgong?!" cried Charlotte. "I think the Ditto misheard you."

"It didn't mishear me at all," Sarah said with a knowing smile.

"But . . . but . . . we've already got a bunch of Dewgong!" Charlotte cried. Clearly, Sarah's selection made no sense to her.

The Dragonite and the Dewgong began to battle.

"No," cried Skip, running over to the gym. "Ditto, my sister made a mistake. She told you to morph into—"

"Quiet, Skip!" Sarah called. "It's too late. The fight has already begun."

The Dragonite began to use Steel Wing on the Dewgong. The Dewgong absorbed the damage well, and struck back with Ice Shard, landing several satisfying blows. The Dragonite recovered and continued to attack. Both Pokémon were building up to more powerful charge attacks. In the race to be first, the Dragonite won. It shot a blistering Hyper Beam straight at the Dewgong. The beam connected and sent the water-type Pokémon reeling across the mat. It did not fall over, but it was clear to everyone watching that the Dewgong was badly wounded.

"Oh no," cried Charlotte. "It's all over. We're going to lose for sure!"

"I'm not so certain about that," Sarah said confidently.

The injured Dewgong hit the Dragonite with two more Ice Shards, then squared off for a charge attack. What happened next was beyond what anyone—including Sarah—was expecting.

The Dewgong let loose a Blizzard move. To call it a *move* did not really do the attack justice. It was the most powerful Blizzard that had ever been launched by any Dewgong—real or imitated—in the history of the game of Pokémon. If regular charge attacks were airplanes, then this charge was a spaceship. It hit the Dragonite with the full force of an actual blizzard. It caused snow and ice to form—not just around the gym, but over half the island. Everyone watching the match was momentarily blinded by a flurry of ice crystals.

When Sarah could see again, the Dewgong was standing alone in the gym with a big smile on its face. The Dragonite was nowhere to be found. At least, for a moment. Soon, Sarah realized that a large, rectangular block of ice off to the side of the ring was, in fact, the Dragonite. It had been encased in ice and snow. As Sarah watched, the block slowly fell over onto its side. Then the ice broke open to reveal a frost-covered Dragonite, now unconscious.

"We won!" shouted Skip. "Holy cats, we won!"

"Yessss," said Sarah, pumping her fist.

The Pokémon trainers on the opposing team let their mouths hang open in surprise. They had been defeated, and couldn't quite believe it. One of them hung his head in shame.

"But how did you know?" Charlotte asked Sarah. "How did you know the Ditto could turn itself into such a powerful Dewgong?"

"I didn't," Sarah answered matter-of-factly.

Charlotte was confused

"But you told it what form to take, right?" Charlotte pressed.

"No," said Sarah. "I didn't do that, either. See, I was wondering what form I should have it use . . . and then I started thinking about my mom."

"About your *mom*?" Charlotte asked skeptically.

Sarah nodded. "I'm always asking her to let me make more of my own decisions. You know, to let me choose what *I* want to do. She lets me do that a little—more than she lets Skip, anyway."

"That's true," said Skip. "You may think I don't notice that, but I do."

"Anyhow, I thought to myself, if I'm all for people getting to make their own decisions . . . maybe I should let the Ditto decide for itself."

"What?" said Charlotte. "I've never heard of anybody doing that."

"I hadn't, either, to be honest with you," said Sarah. "But I thought it was worth a shot. The Ditto *knew* it could make a Dewgong with an incredibly powerful Blizzard. If I hadn't let it choose its own form, I never would have found out."

Suddenly, the sky above them began to grow dark. For a moment, Sarah was worried.

"Is it sunset already?" she asked. "What's going on?"

"I think the game is ending," said Skip with a smile.

One by one, the PokéStops and gyms across the island winked-out like streetlights being extinguished at dawn. They sky continued to darken. Soon, there was only a single source of light remaining on the entire island—an eerie green glow coming from the central-most clearing. Drawn like moths to a flame, Sarah, Skip, and Charlotte wandered toward it. So did the opposing Pokémon trainers.

Arriving at the clearing, they saw Alice there waiting for them. She was standing beside the strange lamp where the green fire still burned. She had a big grin on her face, and looked about ten years younger. The Pokémon trainer who acted as spokesman for the aliens was there, too. He looked decidedly less pleased.

"You did it!" Alice shouted. She ran over to the Sarah, Skip, and Charlotte, and hugged them all at once. She was a surprisingly strong hugger.

"Mmph," said Skip. "I'm being smothered."

"You really did it!" Alice said again, releasing them. "I'm so proud of all of you. Our world will be safe for another thirty years."

Sarah spied Richard, Sammy, and Maria standing together at the side of the clearing. They also looked pleased and relieved. Richard gave them all a thumbs-up.

The other Pokémon trainer cleared his throat. "We're really not so bad, you know. You should consider letting us in to your world anyway. You might get to like us once you got to know us."

Alice looked down her nose. "We both know that's not true," she told him.

The Pokémon trainer shrugged and smiled as if to say, *Hey, it was worth a shot.*

"A deal's a deal, even if it's hundreds of years old," Alice reminded him.

"I know," he said sheepishly. "Maybe I'll see you again in another thirty years."

"Could be," said Alice. "Could be."

The spokesman then turned to the six Pokémon trainers from his own side. They, too, had filed into the clearing. The spokesman's expression became much more stern.

"I will not take any more of your time," he said to Alice, though his gaze never left his troops. "I will return to our home and deal with these . . . *disappointments* presently."

Sarah was reminded again that these aliens were not nice people, and felt all the more pleased to have helped to keep them from her planet.

"One more thing before you go," said Alice. "Don't forget that we made an *amendment* to our regular bargain. I'm sure you intend to honor your side of it."

"We do," said the Pokémon trainer.

"Very well," said Alice. "Then I will be in touch."

The trainer nodded.

"Come children," Alice said. "Back to the beach. It's awfully late at night in our world, and you all have school tomorrow."

They followed Alice out of the clearing and into the woods, heading for the western shore of the island. A few footsteps inside the tree line, and they heard a sound like a thunderclap and the mysterious green flame behind them was extinguished. Sarah did not look back, but knew that the visitors had departed.

In just a couple of minutes, they reached the beach. Alice's boat was still there. There was also a second boat a few yards down the beach that Sarah hadn't noticed before. Richard, Sammy, and Maria sheepishly filed into it and cast off for the mainland.

"I hope the three of you have learned a lesson about sticking your nose into other people's business," Alice called after them.

"Yes," Richard called back. "Sorry about that. We won't do it again."

"I should hope not," Alice said.

The rest of them climbed aboard Alice's boat and began rowing back across the water in the direction of Sarah and Skip's house. Sarah looked up at Alice. Deep tranquility had spread across her ancient features.

"I have a question," Sarah said. "From what you said before, it sounds like maybe you played against the aliens yourself. Is that right?"

Alice nodded. "It was very long ago."

"Were you scared?" Sarah asked.

"Of course I was. And I didn't even have teammates. Me playing horseshoes against an alien to determine the future of Earth."

"Well, so . . . how did you feel after?" Sarah asked. "Because I'm not sure how I should feel just now. So much just happened. I kind of can't take it all in."

"Don't worry," said Alice. "That's normal. Later, when you've had time to process these events, the thing I hope you'll take away from this is that excellence and hard work matters. You just did something that involved a lot of hard work, and which showed a lot of excellence on your part. And the thing about excellence is that it's contagious. It doesn't want to be contained. It's liable to seep from one area of your life into another. Excellence at something that is 'just a game'—even if you don't use it to save the world—can translate to excellence in school, in work, and in your community. A habit of being excellent is a good habit to have."

"I think I understand," said Sarah. "Thanks."

Alice nodded.

And with that, the bottom of the boat scraped against the rocky shoreline. They had reached land.

"Now get back in your beds before your mother wakes up," Alice urged. "I'll see that Charlotte gets home safely."

"Wait, I have another question before we go," said Sarah. "What was the extra bargain you made with those aliens? The thing that convinced them to play again, even though they'd already beaten Richard and the others?

"Ahh," said Alice. "An old trick. I simply offered them whatever was in my power to grant them."

"In addition to their getting to invade our world and make it lousy," said Sarah.

"That's right," said Alice.

"And what did they offer in return?" Sarah asked.

"The very same thing," Alice said. "I was going to talk to you about this later, but now may be as good a time as any. I think that the request should be yours, Sarah. You showed extraordinary leadership and bravery during the contest. I think that *you* should be the one to ask for a special favor."

"Oh," said Sarah, a bit stunned. "What should I ask for?"

"Anything you want," Alice said. "Whatever pops into your head first is probably the right answer. Trust your instincts."

"Okay then," said Sarah. "I've got it."

Sarah leaned in close and whispered her request into Alice's ear.

Alice leaned back in the boat and smiled.

"I think that's a very fine favor indeed," Alice said. "And I'm certain it's something they will be able to provide."

"What?" asked Skip excitedly. "What did you wish for?"

"Ah, ah," said Alice. "If you tell everyone, it might not come true."

Alice flashed Sarah the tiniest of winks.

She smiled. "Yeah," she said to her brother. "I should keep it private."

"But I wanna *know*!" Skip howled.

"Then you'll just have to wait," she said. And with that, Sarah hopped out of the boat and onto the rocky shore. She gave Skip a look that asked if he was coming or not.

Skip climbed from the boat and onto dry land.

"See you at school tomorrow," Sarah called to Charlotte.

"Oh, yeah," Charlotte said. "School. It's weird to think about that. Even after you save the world from alien invaders, you still have to do stuff like go to school."

"Tell me about it," said Alice, as she began rowing back down the shoreline in the direction of Charlotte's house.

"Are you *really* not going to tell me what you wished for?" Skip asked as he and Sarah began the climb up the rocky path toward their house.

Sarah didn't even respond. She was far too excited.

PART EIGHT

The next day passed in a blur, mostly because Sarah had been too exhilarated to sleep, and was drowsy through all of her classes. When she saw Charlotte at lunch, they only chatted briefly.

"Did you get home all right?" Sarah asked.

"Yeah," said Charlotte. "My parents had no idea I'd been out all night. The fact that they didn't find out makes it feel even more like a weird dream."

"I totally know what you mean," Sarah responded. "It's almost like it didn't really happen."

But after school, something happened that made it seem not like a dream at all.

Sarah and Skip trekked the now-familiar route home from school together, playing Pokémon GO along the way. For whatever reason, knowing that she had just saved the known-world by playing Pokémon GO—*and* knowing that she was the top player in the world—did not dim Sarah's desire to play the game in any way. Hitting those PokéStops and catching a couple of Meowth still seemed like a great thing to do on the walk home.

When they arrived at their house, their mother was out on the front porch waiting for them. She was drinking a cup of tea and had a bright smile on her face. In fact, Sarah couldn't remember her mother ever looking so pleased.

"Kids!" she called as soon as they were in earshot. "You're not going to believe what happened today! It's the most wonderful, fantastic, unbelievable thing!"

"What is it?" asked Skip.

Sara remained thoughtfully silent.

"It's my quilt shop!" their mother said. "When I arrived to open up today, there was a long line of people already standing outside, waiting. I couldn't believe it! At first, I thought there must be some kind of mistake. But when I unlocked the door, they started to come inside. They were very orderly and patient, but they all wanted to buy quilts. Lots and lots of quilts."

"Cool!" Skip said enthusiastically.

"And that wasn't even the strangest thing," their mother continued. "I think that Pokémon GO must really be catching on . . . because they were all dressed like Pokémon trainers. They had the hats and backpacks and everything. I also think they might have been related somehow, because they had gray eyes. I'd never seen that before. It must run in the family."

"I guess it must," said Sarah with a knowing grin.

"The first customer bought *every* quilt I had in the shop!" her mother continued. "Each of the others ordered at least twenty more quilts. I'll be quilting for years just to fill all of the orders I took today."

"Is that a bad thing?" Skip asked. "Will it be too much work?"

"No, it's a *wonderful* thing," their mother said. "My shop is going to be so successful now. I might even be able to afford to hire staff. This is great!"

"I'm glad to hear you had such a good day," Sarah said after a yawn.

"Why are you so sleepy?" Mom asked.

"I guess you might say it's been an eventful twenty-four hours," Sarah replied.

"Well, here's something that ought to pep you up again," her mother said. "With all the money I made selling quilts today, I got a little present for you and Skip. It's out in the garage if you want to take a look."

Sarah and Skip looked at each other for a moment, then raced off in the direction of the garage. Their mother plodded after them, trying not to spill her tea. Sarah pressed the button to open the automatic door. It slowly raised to reveal a brand new rowboat with oars, life jackets, and a dolly with wheels for pulling it down to the water.

"Wow, thank you!" Sarah shouted.

"Thanks mom!" called Skip.

"Now you'll be able to go and play on the island whenever you like," their mother said. "As long as you stick together and get permission from an adult."

"We promise to," Skip said.

"Yes, we promise," added Sarah.

"And Skip," their mother continued, "I haven't forgotten about you wanting a basketball hoop, too. This weekend, some workmen are going to come install a brand new hoop and backboard in our driveway."

"Awesome!" said Skip. He jumped up and down with excitement.

"So, what do you think?" their mother asked. "Wanna take your new boat out for a spin this afternoon?"

Sarah yawned again. "Actually, I think I might like to have a nap. I might even go to bed early."

Were it not for the wind in the trees and the lapping of the water down on the beach, you could have heard a pin drop.

"Sarah, are you all right?" her mother asked, puzzled. "You're not getting sick are you? Is there a bug going around at school?"

She leaned over to feel her daughter's forehead.

"I'm fine, Mom," Sara said. "Just sleepy. Am I not allowed to be sleepy every once in a while?"

"I suppose so," her mother answered cautiously. "Okay. Go have a nap."

"Thanks," said Sarah, and she headed inside the house and straight to her bedroom. She took off her backpack, removed her shoes, and fell head-first into bed.

That night, Sarah dreamed of the island once again. She dreamed that she was standing on the coast, looking back at her own house. It was the middle of the day and the sun was shining brightly. The air was cool and filled with mist from the sea. After a moment, Sarah heard a rustling and realized she had been joined by someone—or something—on the coast beside her. She glanced over and saw a familiar face.

With a very long tongue.

"Hey, there," Sarah said to the Lickitung.

"Hey, yourself," it said.

"What are you doing here?" Sarah asked the Pokémon. "This is my dream."

"I came to say thank you for everything you did," said the Lickitung.

"I should be thanking you," Sarah said. "If you hadn't helped me find the Ancient Venomoth, I might never have known I had the Ditto. And then everything could have gone very differently."

"Well, we can just thank each other then," said the Lickitung.

Sarah decided this might be the best approach.

"Will I ever get to see you again?" she asked. "Will I ever get to see any of the Pokémon again?"

"I don't know," said the Lickitung. "This island is a strange place where worlds connect. There won't be another contest between humans and those aliens here for many years. You'll practically be middle-aged when it happens again! Still, there might be other ways we could see each other again. They say you should never say never. Humans say that, anyway. If you look hard enough, you just may see another Pokémon one day."

"That sounds awesome," Sarah said. "I hope so. In the meantime, I guess I'll just have to keep playing Pokémon GO."

"Is that so bad?" asked the Lickitung.

"Not at all," said Sarah. "It's actually really, really fun."

"Oh," said the Lickitung with a smile. "Good."

They stayed like that, standing on the beach together, looking back toward the mainland.

When Sarah woke the next morning, she felt more well-rested than she could ever remember being. She made her way downstairs for breakfast. Her mother and Skip weren't yet awake. Sarah poured herself a tall, cool glass of orange juice. As she drank it, she strolled around the house, and found herself walking to her mother's quilting room so she could look out the window and watch the sun rising over the island.

As Sarah looked on, she saw a flicker of movement among the island's trees. She sipped her orange juice. It was almost certainly the wind attempting to pull the last of the leaves from their branches. Or a small forest animal. Or a trick of the light.

But Sarah let herself wonder. And hope.

Maybe her adventures with the Pokémon were only just beginning.

A smile spread across her face. Then she heard the familiar sound of Skip's feet padding above her on the second floor. She finished her OJ and made her way back to the kitchen to help prepare breakfast. It was time to start the day.

Do you Love pLaying Pokémon GO?

Check out these books for fans of Pokémon GO!

Catching the
Jigglypuff Thief
ALEX POLAN

Following Meowth's
Footprints
ALEX POLAN

Chasing
Butterfree
ALEX POLAN

Cracking the
Magikarp Code
ALEX POLAN

Available wherever books are sold!

ABOUT THE AUTHOR

Ken A. Moore is national bestselling author who
plays entirely too much Pokémon GO!